Quest for the

Firebird

Quest for the Firebird

Firebird

Book 4 in the Valdeor Chronicles

Sandralena Hanley

Other Books by Sandralena Hanley

Valdeor Chronicles

Book One: Champion of Valdeor

Book Two: Waykeepers of Valdeor

Book Three: Pilgrims of Valdeor

Royal Rescue series, for adults

The Stolen Princess

Quest for the Firebird

Copyright ©2025 Sandra L. Hanley

All rights reserved.

Printed in the United States of America

Cover by Emily Anne Hickman

Edited by Susan P. Peek

Formatted by Havelah McLat

ISBN: 978-1-7377398-4-5

Table of Contents

Dedication

To my sister Susie, a published author, who told me she knew I had a book in me. Her encouragement is what started my writing journey.

Through the Resurrection, All things are renewed.

Family Tree Chart

Mintala:

Reina Lauressa & Prince Consort Alloryn

Princess Lauryn & Prince Allyn (twins), 17

Prince Jarell, 15

Prince Allek & Princess Allyria (twins), 12

Princess Lysa, 6

Samarantha:

Prince Gensard & Princess Jiana

Princess Giada, 15

Prince Micah, 14

Princess Rialla, 12

Winterhome:

Prince Everard I & Princess Marissa

Prince Arden, 24

Prince Everard II, 20

Princess Mariade, 14

Canteor:

Queen Sefira & Prince Consort Leander

Prince Xylander, 17

Prince Andro, 15

Princess Leanna, 13

Maps

VALDEOR

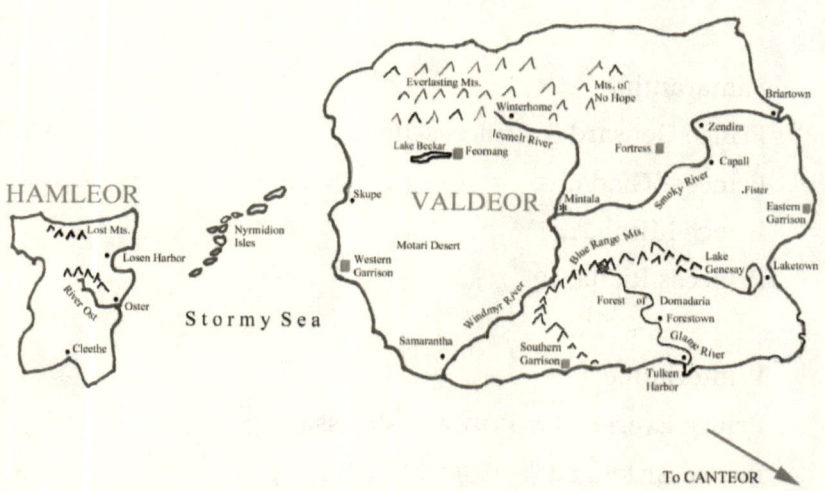

HAMLEOR

Lost Mts.

Losen Harbor

River Ost

Oster

Cleethe

Nyrmidion
Isles

Stormy Sea

Everlasting Mts.

Mts. of
No Hope

Winterhome

Icemelt River

Lake Beckar

Feornang

Fortress

Zendira

Briartown

Capall

Skupe

VALDEOR

Mintala

Smoky River

.Fister

Eastern
Garrison

Motari Desert

Western
Garrison

Blue Range Mts.

Lake
Genesay

Laketown

Windmyr River

Forest of

Domadaria

Forestown

Samarantha

Southern
Garrison

Glade River

Tulken
Harbor

To CANTEOR

CANTEOR

Bidori Cressava Isle of Origin

Sikarta

Tilmuk

Caervale

Merione Mts.

JUGARA DESERT

Dabbori

Radhir

Uludra

Kiwan

Zarde Heights

Impiri

1 Quest

Mother, known to the rest of the world as Reina Lauressa, Valdeor's ruler, lay on a chaise lounge Father had pulled onto the balcony. Even though the mild spring sun shone on her, she was bundled up under a heap of blankets. She had some gray streaks in her chestnut brown hair, and laugh lines at the corner of her eyes. But new lines caused by pain drew her lips down.

The family gathered around her. Father, Prince Consort Alloryn, sat on a chair beside her, his hand clasping hers. Care sat heavy on his broad shoulders, making him look older than his forty years. He gazed sorrowfully at his queen and bride.

Lauryn, the firstborn, together with her twin brother Allyn, age seventeen, leaned on the parapet. Her younger brother Jarell, fifteen, stood with his arms crossed. The youngest twins, Allyria and Allek, twelve, sat at Mother's feet. Lysa, age six, leaned against Father's leg. Even the family dog, Trekker the third, lay beside Mother's couch.

"Your mother and I have gathered you here for a family meeting. It is time to talk about Valdeor's next ruler."

Lauryn's heart clenched. Mother must be seriously ill if they were having this conversation. Yet, wasn't she the heir? A few months shy of eighteen, she'd always believed that Mother would name her the crown princess on her birthday.

"Is mother dying?" Lysa gasped.

"I thought Lauryn would become the next queen. She's the oldest." Allyn mused.

"Aren't you going to rule, Father?" Jarell inquired.

Mother raised her hand, palm out, and the children grew silent. "I may recover from this illness, that lasted all winter, if the One Who Fashioned All wills it. But the Noble Council thought it best to plan for the future. It isn't too soon for my successor to take on a more active role before becoming our kingdom's leader."

Father said, "The Council of Nobles have asked us to gather in the throne room to test Lauryn and Allyn's virtues. The sun is at its highest and the heartstones are at the height of their power."

Father picked Mother up and led them to the throne room where the nobles had already taken their seats.

The six heartstones of virtues scattered their

rainbow colors through the room as the noon sun shone overhead. Ruby for courage. Sapphire for wisdom. Topaz for justice. Emerald for moderation. Amethyst for faith. Citrine for hope. And on a pedestal in the center of the room was a diamond for love. Not romantic love, but charity for all.

"Let us see if the heartstones indicate that Lauryn has the virtues to be Valdeor's next ruler," Mother announced.

Mother beckoned Lauryn to come closer. She bent her head. Mother removed the medallion from her neck and placed it over Lauryn's shoulders. She walked over and stood before the diamond pedestal where the light beams converged.

The stones on the medallion lit up with the rainbow-colors of the heartstones.

Lauryn swallowed. She had demonstrated every virtue needed for a ruler.

A rustling of whispers came from the benches where the nobility sat.

She returned to Mother, took off the medallion, and handed it back to her.

Mother asked Allyn to approach. Her twin bent down and Mother put it over his head. Once the medallion rested on his breast, all the stones shone, some brighter than others. Just as it did for her.

Confusion washed over Lauryn. Glancing around,

she saw the same reaction on everyone's faces, including Allyn. What did it mean?

The noble councilors exclaimed and broke out in conversations. Some argued among themselves and others called on Mother for a solution.

Mother used her power as Reina, standing and raising her hand for silence. She called for the Council to convene in her private audience hall for discussion on the matter.

Once they were dismissed, her brother told Lauryn he was headed for the training ground. "I need a good bout with a sword to settle my disquiet. I'll seek out my best friend in the guards and challenge him." Lauryn wished she had something physical to do to burn off energy.

Two days later, Father made an announcement after the family finished the midday meal. "The oldest twins have spent time with us in the judgment hall. They have the basic training of a ruler. But the Noble Council approached your mother with a plan. Whoever can win the contest they devised will take over more of your mother's duties." Father looked pointedly at Lauryn and Allyn.

"What sort of contest, Father?" Allyn took after Father with dark hair and broad shoulders. Allyn had Father's handsome features, which was the bane of his life. Lauryn took every opportunity to tease him because the young noble ladies swooned over him.

"Your mother's medallion showed you both have virtues needed to be a good ruler. We've talked it over with the council and agreed a quest is the way to prove which eldest twin should sit upon the throne. Not only finding the quest's object, but also your actions during the journey, will determine your fitness as ruler."

Lauryn moved to take her mother's free hand. She knew that she looked like a female version of her twin, yet shared her mother's slender figure and chestnut-colored hair. She had what she termed a beauty spot at her left eyebrow's corner. Her brothers unkindly referred to it as a mole.

She glanced between her parents. "So it's a contest between Allyn and me?" Her voice sounded clipped in her own ears. She couldn't contain her disappointment.

Resentment burned a hole in her chest. She was the firstborn. She had studied diplomacy, law, and history since she was nine. She expected to follow in her mother's footprints. Allyn wasn't as studious as she. She believed her parents hadn't pushed him as hard as they pushed her. Yet they would allow him the place she had worked for her whole life? Had she not impressed the Noble Council with her diligence?

Although she never doubted the crown would eventually be hers, she had striven to show she was the best choice. And now the council put her on the same level as Allyn. He had natural charm, but wasn't as responsible as she was. He excelled in fighting and hunting.

"Essentially, yes." Mother's penetrating gaze seemed to see the struggle in Lauryn's soul. "A ruler must have virtues, beyond being born first. Book learning doesn't make one a good ruler. It's the ability to make the best decisions for your country over your own desires. Choosing the right thing to do is hard. A quest will give you a chance to make real-life decisions and live with the consequences."

Lauryn dropped her eyes. Although she didn't like it, she understood Mother had agreed to this plan because she wanted the best ruler for her people.

"You wouldn't send them off without a mentor." Jarell piped up. "Who is it to be? Captain Rodrek? Or Uncle Guy and Aunt Donella? Everard? Someone has to keep them accountable. What if they try to cheat?" Jarell's looks favored Mother. His chestnut brown hair had a perpetual curl in it. He couldn't bother to have the royal barber cut it as frequently as Allyn did.

Ugh! A babysitter? Lauryn hoped not.

Before Mother or Father could answer, Allek piped up. He was short for his age. He looked like an angel with dirty blonde curls, but he tumbled in and out of trouble. "Are they going to find a sword like you did, Father? Or maybe a dragon's hoard?"

"There's no such things as dragons, Allek. They are only in picture books," his twin Allyria chided him.

"You would know. You always have your nose in a book," he flung back.

Ignoring him, Allyria continued, "The only monster found in Valdeor was the kratigula. And Father already slew him to gain the Crestin sword."

The siblings descended into a squabble on what constituted a monster, whether a sea monster or the dreadful lagators or hippogrif of Canteor counted.

"A firebird's feather." Their mother's voice cut across the argument. "They need to bring back a firebird's feather."

They all turned toward her, astonishment on their faces.

"Do firebirds even exist?" Allyn crossed his arms, his eyebrows winging up more than usual with surprise.

"Legend says that it lives on the highest mountains. I read it in one of my books," Allyria announced in the silence that followed.

After the family conclave dispersed, the two sets of twins, Allyn and Lauryn, Allek and Allyria, as well as Jarell, gathered in the library. Bookshelves, made of dark exotic wood, spanned the walls from floor to ceiling. Comfortable chairs dotted the room and window seats nestled invitingly in two walls.

"A quest of our own, like Father and Mother had before Mother claimed the throne!" Allyn sounded excited.

"But it won't be all fun," Lauryn, ever practical, declared. "They had help along the way. And Father trained under the warrior Justinian, the greatest swordsman."

"Father has taught me well, if that is what you are implying." Allyn put his hands on his hips and glared at his twin. "I can handle the brawn."

"Then I need to come along, too, to be the brains." Jarell ran his hand along books on the shelves.

"Ha. We don't need a tinkerer to find a legendary creature." Allyn raised an eyebrow.

"But you will be glad of my sword to face monsters." Jarell crossed his arms. "You know Brant the weapons master said that I have talent nearly equal to Father and you."

"But not as adept as my best friend, Everard," Allyn challenged. "He'll soon be a royal guard."

Lauryn impatiently tapped a foot while the boys traded insults. Not a promising start.

Out of the corner of her eye, she saw movement. Allek held a ladder while Allyria climbed to the top. Their younger sister tugged a large tome off the shelf, too big for her to handle. Allyria teetered, trying to hold onto the book as it slipped from her grasp.

"Allyria!" Lauryn raced for her, but Allyn, who was closer, beat her to the rescue. He caught their sister as she toppled from the ladder.

Lauryn oomphed as Allyria's tome hit her. She would have tumbled backwards if Jarell hadn't braced her from behind.

"What was that all about?" Allyn chided Allyria as he set her down.

Unruffled, Allyria pushed herself free of Allyn's hold and calmly rescued the book at Lauryn's feet. "I figured you'd want to see this book on magical creatures."

In silence, they all followed Allyria to a table where she laid it down for their inspection. The tooled leather cover depicted an engraved griffin. She carefully opened it to the title page. "Monsters of Legend and Myth: a Study from Many Lands" was the imposing title in fancy lettering.

They all leaned over her as she gently turned the ancient, browned pages. Allyria flipped past the kratigula, griffin, hippogrif, camelopardalis, lagator, draco, and nixie, until she came to the firebird. The illustrator had colored the bird in all its glory. The purplish-red feathers were tipped with golden wings. It had a feathery crest on its head similar to a rooster. The talons were gold-colored.

Allyria read aloud, "The phoenix, or firebird, nests in

the mountains. After five hundred years, the female lays an egg. Once that is done, the old firebird bursts into flames. While the ashes are still hot, the bird rises again. Leaving the egg in the nest, the phoenix seeks a new home. The bird is very rare. It is of mild temperament, unless it feels its egg is threatened. Then beware, O Traveler, their sharp beaks and claws."

"What does 'tem-per-tent' mean?" Allek drummed his fingers on the table.

"Temperament. It means a person or animal's traits. Personality. You'd know if you paid better attention to your lessons." Allyn spoke patronizingly.

Allek disliked his siblings' tendency to treat him like a child because he had a round, angelic-looking face and curls. Huffing, he drifted away from the table.

"Hmm. Now we know what it looks like and some of its habits, but how do we find it?" Lauryn tossed her hair and sat on a cushioned chair.

"I'm not sure it even exists." Allyn perched on the matching chair's armrest. "The book is about myths. I wonder if this is a wild goose chase, meant to prove we have the perseverance to scale mountains, and are worthy of battle."

"You mean a wild firebird chase," Jarell said. They all groaned at his pun.

"But if we possess only prowess in tracking, hunting, and battle, how does that prove one of us a better ruler?"

Lauryn turned her head toward her twin. "You would easily win. I'm a fair archer, and trained by Captain Rodrek in defensive tactics and tracking, too. But I can't beat you in hand-to-hand combat. I can't race you to a mountain top. No, this is about responsibility. Or didn't you listen to what Mother said?"

"That's it!" Jarell smirked. They all stared at him.

"What are you talking about?" Lauryn frowned.

"We know where to start the search for the firebird. We've listened to the answer hundreds of times." He beamed at their astonished looks.

"Quit being mysterious," Allyn urged, impatiently.

"How did Father find Mother in hiding at the time of the civil war?" Jarell rocked on the balls of his feet, mischievous enjoyment written all over his face.

The older twins exchanged puzzled glances.

Allek's voice drifted down from above their heads. "The mirror pool in the heart of the Lost Mountains."

Lauryn spun in her seat until she spied Allek sitting on the fifteen-foot-tall book ladder's top rung.

"Of course!" Allyn snapped his fingers and leapt up. He slapped Jarell on the back. "Good thinking! It's said one can see the object one searches for in the pool. We'll start there."

Lauryn frowned up at Allek. "What are you doing up there? Mother won't be pleased if you fall."

Allek rolled his eyes. "I'm waiting for Allyria to tell

me where to find the next book, of course." Lauryn recognized the twin mind-reading that she occasionally shared with Allyn.

Before Lauryn could ask which book, Allyria trotted to the ladder where her twin perched and rolled it halfway around the room. "The book with the red cover on the third shelf from the top, Allek."

Plucking the leather-bound book from the shelf, he jumped when halfway down the ladder.

When Allyria moved aside the first book and opened the new one, Lauryn shared an impressed glance with her twin. "Lands of Myth and Magic, a True History" the title page read.

"Looks like the same author as the last book to me." Jarell chuckled.

The first entry was the Isle of Origin.

"Uncle Guy and Aunt Donella already found this one." Allyria licked her finger and turned the thick vellum page.

The Mirror Pool of Desire was the second entry. Allyria read aloud, "Found in Hamleor's Lost Mountain Range. The entrance is through the Moon Canyon, which is thought to be in the shape of a crescent moon. Or perhaps, Dear Reader, only found on the night of a full moon. The author of this work has not verified the veracity of these statements."

"I bet he hasn't verified the veracity of any of these

legends," Jarell wryly said. "He sounds too prosy to leave his archives and go adventuring."

Allyn shushed him and motioned Allyria to keep reading.

"In the mountain's deepest heart is a cave with gems so beautiful, it blinds one to all else but the desire to possess its wealth. Legend is that the ancients mined the heartstones, the most brilliant of gems, here. If one can avoid the allure of vast wealth, they must seek the mirror-like pond at the cave's center. Anyone who gazes into it will see their heart's desire."

"Heart's desire?" Jarell snorted. "It sounds like a place for lovesick mooncalves." He clasped his hands together dramatically, batted his eyelashes, and sighed, "Drink of the magical water to dream of your true love."

Allyn and Lauryn punched his shoulders from either side. "Ow!" Jarell gave them a fake wounded look.

Allyria closed the book. "Well, it worked for Father, didn't it?"

Lauryn pushed away the image it conjured of her father as a lovesick dolt. Even middle-aged, he was a warrior to be reckoned with.

Over dinner, Allyn told Father about their discoveries, with his siblings eagerly chiming in. Mother ate in her chambers, too tired to join them.

"Who gets to go on the quest? Only Lauryn and Allyn?" Jarell pushed a lock of hair off his forehead.

Father paused in slicing his lamb cutlet. "Your mother and I think you three eldest are up to the trek."

Trekker, descendant of the original wolfhound who accompanied Father on his travels, lifted his head at his name. Allyn secretly slipped the dog a piece of meat under the table.

Jarell puffed out his chest and attacked his lamb and potatoes with gusto.

Allyn's tension drained at the thought of his brother joining them. Jarell would have his back in a fight. His brother wouldn't desire to usurp the throne, but he loved a good adventure.

Jarell, the third child, tinkered forever with contraptions. He could be found with the master armorer or the town blacksmith. His room looked like a workshop, filled with projects.

He could help Allyn to look after their sister. Not that she was defenseless. Father taught all of them how to defend themselves with protective moves and weapons. Lauryn preferred throwing daggers, while the boys trained with swords. The three of them together had a better chance of succeeding.

Allek surreptitiously flicked a pea at Allyn, which Allyn interpreted as jealousy at not getting to go, too.

"I will copy out the pages from the two books we

found today and draw a map to the cave of gems for you." Allyria cut her meat and vegetables in small, dainty pieces.

"I'll help Jarell make weapons for killing monsters." Allek announced.

"No, you won't. You're too impulsive. Leave it to the experts." Jarell glared at him.

From Jarell's smothered yelp, Allyn was pretty sure Allek had kicked Jarell under the table. Allyn gave Lauryn a look, and she presumably interpreted correctly and kicked Allek on his other side because he let out an oomph.

"How is Mother?" Allyria, the diplomatic one, changed the conversation.

"As well as can be expected. She doesn't want you to worry." Father had aged in the months since Mother's health began to decline.

Lysa, the youngest, rapidly blinked her eyes.

Father noticed and patted her hand.

He regained his focus, glancing between the three eldest. "Guy and Donella are coming. They will help you on your journey's first leg. Be packed and ready to leave the day after tomorrow."

"That means we get to travel by portal." Lauryn grinned.

Not only was portal travel more exciting, but Allyn knew the reason for her relief. He loved sailing, but she wasn't fond of it. Normally, a trip across the Stormy Seas took three weeks.

He stared at his father wondering if he was trying to allay their fears for their mother. Why else would he shorten the quest before it began? Allyn's heart sank. Mother must be in a very bad way.

He loved a good challenge but he had no desire to rule the kingdom. Lauryn had prepared her whole life for that. Allyn would rather raise his sword in the realm's defense, heading the army.

But a king's day-to-day affairs? He'd gladly pass. He liked his freedom too much. The freedom to come and go from the palace. The freedom to travel to other provinces. As ruler he wouldn't have the same options.

He wasn't ready to be High King, nor did he think Lauryn was ready to be Reina. But she was more qualified for it than he was.

He groaned internally at the thought of all the studying he'd need to do if he became the crown prince. He'd rather be on the training grounds with his best friend, Everard.

They had been friends since childhood. Ever—Prince Everard II—was the prince of Winterhome's second son. Everard was four years older, and learning to be a royal guard. Allyn knew that Ever hoped one day to be assigned to the royal family, preferably Allyn's own personal guard.

Jarell followed Allyn to his room and they spent the evening discussing the upcoming trip. Jarell certainly needn't worry about winning. He was more interested in deciding all the useful items he could bring.

No doubt Lauryn was the only one truly determined to prove herself capable of leading Valdeor.

Allyn would go from a sense of duty. He wouldn't let his parents down.

2 Portal

At the named time, Lauryn stood in the Entry Hall with her belongings in a satchel at her feet. She wore a leather dress that fell to her knees and leggings underneath, topped off with sturdy boots. Her belt was strapped over her dress. She had pulled the sides of her hair into two small braids which she tied in the back, keeping it out of her eyes.

She glanced around the familiar room in the morning light.

Allyn stood a few feet away talking in hushed tones with Jarell. They both showed signs of eagerness to get started.

Father stood beside Mother, who sat in a chair the servants had brought for her.

Fighting the sick feeling in the pit of her stomach, Lauryn took inventory of her belongings for the third time since arriving downstairs. Dagger tucked in her belt. A tiny knife hidden in her elaborate hair barrette. A pouch holding coins in a deep pocket of her leather skirt. Three throwing knives in her satchel's main compartment, as well as a waterskin, a length of lightweight yet tough rope, and dried food for several days.

Allek sidled up to her and held out a clenched hand. Unsure of what he might give her, her stomach tightened in fear of a lizard, although it was likely to be smaller, like a beetle. But considering the circumstances, he would probably offer her something useful. She extended her hand and he put something cold into it.

She stared at a small black rock, one end pointed, tied on a string.

"It's a lodestone." He answered her puzzled expression. "It will always point true north." He showed her how it spun until the pointed end faced north.

"Thank you, Allek. You're very thoughtful." She resisted the urge to give him a hug, knowing he would hate it.

Allyria stood behind him. When Allek moved aside, she gave Lauryn two pieces of vellum. One had a hand-printed copy of the descriptions of the Mirror Pool and Firebird. On the other sheet, Allyria had carefully drawn a map of Hamleor's Lost Mountain region. At Allyria's prodding, Lauryn studied the path from Losen Harbor, over the Ost River, to the Moon Canyon marked in red. She recognized Father's handwriting along the page's bottom with exact instructions on how to find it. Relief filled her at the sight.

Hugging Allyria, a hollowness opened in her heart when Lauryn realized it might be months before she returned home.

Lysa appeared at her side next, clutching her favorite

doll. She reached for a hug as well. Tears stained her cheeks. "Come home soon, Lauryn. I'll miss you. I'll keep you, Allyn and Jarell in my nightly prayers."

"Thank you, sweetie pie. I love you, too."

Lysa went to lean against Father's leg. He smoothed out her hair while speaking with Captain Rodrek. Several other royal guardsmen were present, as always.

Lauryn's nervousness returned as the door to the courtyard opened and a couple entered.

As the oldest sibling, Lauryn raised her chin and stepped forward to greet them, pushing down her churning emotions. "Uncle Guy! Aunt Donella! Welcome!" She gave them their honorary title, even though they weren't truly related, and hugged them.

All the siblings followed Lauryn's lead and greeted them.

Then it was time for them to say their goodbyes. Lauryn hugged Father and Mother extra hard.

Lauryn swallowed a lump in her throat. She had a sudden fear that Mother might not live until they returned.

"Safe travels, Daughter," Father whispered in her hair.

"Trust in the One Who Fashioned All," Mother added.

Holding in her tears, Lauryn could only nod and put on a brave face.

Too soon, the group trooped outside the palace, across the courtyard, to the portal.

Many servants and guards had gathered to see them off.

The portal looked like an ordinary garden gate post. One had to look closely to see the triquetra, or interlocking ovals, carved near the top. The same symbol was a birthmark on the back of Uncle Guy's left hand. He and Aunt Donella were Waykeepers, capable of opening the portals and helping wayfarers travel from one portal to another.

Uncle Guy touched his hand to the waypost. Mist curled up from its base, swirling around. An opening in the mist showed a prairie land of waving grasses.

Lauryn had entered the portals with her parents before, but this time was different. The portal seemed like the dark entryway to danger. Her stomach knotted.

"We must make several jumps." Uncle Guy motioned Aunt Donella to lead them through.

Aunt Donella stepped through the mist. Allyn followed her, then Jarell. Excitement and fear warred within Lauryn. She took a deep breath and forced herself forward. Uncle Guy followed on her heels.

The sickening feeling of not knowing which way was up or down, in a gray space, was as bad as Lauryn remembered. The skin of her scalp tightened. She fought the momentary nausea, blinked, and found herself on the grassy plain. Her brothers seemed unaffected by the mode of travel. Making way for Uncle Guy, she spun around and saw no buildings, only a trail leading from one horizon to the other. She barely had time to wonder at the odd placement of a pilgrim's waypost here, before Aunt Donella touched the portal and opened another doorway.

The next landscape was even more forbidding. Lauryn and the others walked into a sandstone canyon baked by the sun. A pool of sulfurous-smelling water bubbled from the canyon wall. Beyond the canyon's end, harsh winds sculpted sand into dunes.

Lauryn shuddered at the thought of becoming stranded in such a barren place. She guessed they stood in the Motari Desert, home to the nomadic tribes.

"Good thing our waterskins have water from the palace cistern." Allyn made a face. "I wouldn't want to have to drink from this."

"If this is early morning, I hate to imagine what the afternoon must feel like." Jarell watched a lizard zip around the rocks.

Perspiration broke out over Lauryn's body. She moved from the blistering heat and stood in the shade. Her brothers followed.

Uncle Guy and Aunt Donella held a low-voiced discussion.

The adults moved away from them. But the canyon's acoustics carried their argument. Uncle Guy wanted to travel to the western garrison. "It is a short jump to the double portal from there."

"But Xylander is visiting his relatives in Samarantha. We should include him."

"I know you think he might be useful, but until the

royals know where the firebird is, he has no place in their group."

Jarell must have overheard too. "Who is Xylander?" he asked Lauryn in an undertone.

Keeping her voice down, she glanced at her brother. "He is Princess Sefira and Prince Consort Leander's oldest son."

"Canteor's crown prince? I wonder why they want him along? Does he also seek the firebird?"

Lauryn had no answer.

Eventually, Aunt Donella won the argument. Uncle Guy grumbled it would add an extra day to the trip. "Four jumps in one day would be too wearing on the body."

He explained it for the siblings. Each jump became more disorienting and induced worse nausea. It was equally hard on the Waykeepers because they expended energy to open the portals. But even more so this time because the last jump would be hundreds of miles over the Stormy Seas to a distant land.

Aunt Donella said that they originally planned to stay overnight at the western garrison and jump to Hamleor the next morning after resting. Now they would stay in Samarantha, the country's southern jewel, with its temperate climate and fertile fields.

Lauryn bubbled with excitement. Princess Giada of Samarantha was her dear friend. She hadn't seen her in two years. Giada had traveled to the palace at Mintala for the twins' fifteenth birthday. They had kept up in letters since then.

Uncle Guy opened the portal and Lauryn eagerly stepped through this time.

After landing outside an inn where the portal doubled as a hitching post, the six travelers made their way to the Samaranthan palace. There Prince Gensard ruled with his consort, Princess Jiana.

The wide boulevards were paved with cobblestones. Palm trees lined the road. As they grew nearer their destination, the gaily-colored houses grew grander with their terracotta red roofs. Lauryn could see lush plants through each courtyard's gates and hear the tinkling fountains. Flowers in window boxes perfumed the air with jasmine and honeysuckle.

The rose-colored stucco palace was cool and airy. She and her siblings had visited it frequently in the winter months. The last time had been two years ago. Samarantha had a much warmer climate, and it was always a treat to have a break from the blowing snow back home.

As they entered the reception hall, Princess Jiana didn't wait for them to be announced. She rushed from her throne and threw her arms around Aunt Donella.

"It's so good to see you, Donella! It's been too long."

Uncle Guy cleared his throat, and she noticed him and hugged him, too.

It took her a moment to recognize the siblings. "Your Highnesses." Princess Jiana curtsied deeply and blushed. "Please excuse my enthusiasm. I haven't seen my old friends in a long time." She looked behind them, no doubt expecting their parents.

"You need not stand on ceremony with us. My parents didn't accompany us." Lauryn smiled at the shy princess. She had once been a slave, rescued by Aunt Donella and Prince Gensard.

Princess Jiana relaxed and smiled. Even now that she was a princess, she still acted awed around other royals.

"My, how you have grown, Jarell. You must've doubled in size." She hugged Jarell, who considered himself at fifteen as too old for hugs. Yet he submitted with good grace. "And sweet Lauryn is prettier than ever!" Lauryn squeezed Princess Jiana back. Allyn forestalled her by sticking out his hand for a handshake.

Princess Jiana motioned to a servant. "Refreshments in the courtyard for our guests."

Soon they sat in Lauryn's favorite chamber in the palace, the inner courtyard. Rose-colored sandstone columns held up a cloister. Lush plants spilled from every corner, some in beds and others sprouting from urns. Heavenly scents filled the air. A rectangular pool dominated the center's large space. On one edge, a stone fountain carved with leaping dolphins spewed water. Lily pads with large white flowers floated in the pool. Orange Koi fish darted under the water.

Servants brought plush cushions and placed them around a low table. Soon, the group sat down in front of covered dishes overflowing with food including figs, pomegranates, dates, apricots, honey cakes, and sugared walnuts. The boys filled their plates high with the delicacies. Lauryn's favorite was the fruit pectin candy sprinkled with confectionery sugar, made from a recipe Princess Jiana had brought with her from her previous mistress.

As soon as they began to eat, Prince Gensard joined them. Lauryn recognized his oldest daughter following in his wake, but not the young man with them. The youngest royals weren't included in the gathering.

The eldest, sweet and pretty Giada, was two years younger than Lauryn and Allyn. She was a younger version of her mother with her blonde, wavy hair, light blue eyes, and sprinkle of freckles.

Allyn froze with an apricot halfway to his mouth when Giada approached. He usually acted very casual with the girls of their acquaintance. But when Giada shyly headed toward a place next to Lauryn, Allyn jumped up and offered her his cushion. He deftly managed to sit beside Giada and engage her in conversation.

Never had Lauryn seen him act this way with her best friend. But Giada was a far cry from when they saw her last at thirteen, when her hair had been in two little-girl braids. Now poised and elegant, draped in silk and jewels, with her hair up, she had blossomed into a lovely young lady.

Lauryn sent an amused look Allyn's way, over Giada's shoulder. He reddened, then studiously ignored his sister.

Lauryn caught Jarell's astonished glance at being abruptly dismissed in the middle of their conversation. *So that's the way it's going to be,* Jarell telegraphed her with a raised eyebrow and resigned expression. Lauryn hid a smile.

Lauryn turned her attention to the young man sitting across from her who seemed about her age. She found him boldly staring at her across the table. Heat flamed in her cheeks. She raised her chin and stared back. He grinned at her, seemingly liking that she challenged him back. She let her lips twitch in a small smile.

"I have been remiss. This is my nephew, Crown Prince Xylander of Canteor." Xylander bowed from the waist as Prince Gensard made the introductions.

Handsome, his skin was a cinnamon color, and he had thick, brown hair. His chocolate eyes seemed to miss nothing as he met her gaze when introduced.

"Wasn't your father a famous gladiator?" Jarell leaned forward, his eyes sparking with interest.

Xylander stiffened. "My father was born a prince of Samarantha. But, yes, he was skilled in the gladiator ring." He seemed both proud and ashamed of his father's prowess.

With their appetites sated and family news shared, Prince Gensard narrowed his eyes at a lull in the conversations. "So, what really brings you here? If it was a pleasurable visit, you would have alerted us in advance. I would assume it isn't a major threat, or Alloryn would have come, not his children. Since you are traveling by portals, it means your errand is urgent. Yet it isn't too dangerous, or the three oldest heirs to the throne wouldn't leave their mother while she is ill." He glanced at the siblings, then the adults, landing last on Aunt Donella.

Lauryn couldn't help but be impressed with the prince's astuteness.

There was something formidable about Prince Gensard. He was still handsome enough that Lauryn could imagine why he had been considered a heart-breaker among her mother's generation. He remained sitting stiffly while everyone else relaxed on floor cushions. But when he glanced at his wife or daughter, his haughty profile softened with fondness.

"You have discerned the crux of the matter. Reina Lauressa knows she approaches her end." Aunt Donella sent apologetic glances at the siblings. "She wishes to secure the succession."

Princess Jiana frowned, glancing from Aunt Donella to her husband. "But isn't Lauryn the heir apparent? The high king's throne is destined for the firstborn, whether boy or girl, I thought."

"Normally, yes," Prince Gensard answered. "Unlike our kingdom, which, by tradition, will pass to our son, Micah. Even though Giada is the eldest at fifteen." Prince Gensard nodded to Aunt Donella to continue.

Instead, Aunt Donella nodded at Lauryn. "This is your story to tell."

All eyes swiveled her way.

Lauryn put on her diplomatic face. "My mother wishes the crown to pass to her most worthy child. Therefore, she has given my brother and me a task. Bring back a firebird's feather."

Prince Gensard frowned. His wife's eyes widened. Oddly enough, Xylander didn't react at all.

Giada piped up, "What is a firebird?"

Allyn jumped in the conversation to explain. "It's a very rare bird. The female only lays an egg every five hundred years. The mother bird is then consumed with fire. But she may rise from the ashes."

Lauryn handed Prince Gensard the description and map, having retrieved them from her satchel. He studied them, then passed them to his wife, then to Giada, and his nephew. Lauryn answered their questions as best as she could.

A sea breeze ruffled Lauryn's hair. She reached up and brushed a strand from her eyes. She stood with her companions on a high cliff. A lone seagull cried overhead. The Stormy Seas sparkled in the sunlight, causing her to squint.

Her palms sweated at the thought of the coming jump.

Hamleor and the Lost Mountains lay far across the water.

Their group had expanded overnight.

Giada had begged her parents to allow her to see her friends off. Lauryn and Allyn had added their pleas. Lauryn because she wanted some time with her friend, and Allyn because, well, he seemed smitten. Giada's parents eventually agreed, on the condition that her personal guard accompany her.

Giada wore a split skirt riding habit. Her golden tresses wound in a braid around her head, making her look older than her fifteen years.

Xylander paced like a caged lion. Remembering Aunt Donella's argument that he be included, Lauryn guessed she had a hidden motive. Though Lauryn was unsure how far he meant to go with them. Did he plan to join their quest?

She had watched everyone's face two nights ago when she spoke about the firebird. All had been surprised or curious. Not Xylander. His expression had closed up when she met his eyes. Had there been speculation there? Or did she imagine it?

If it weren't for Mother's health, Lauryn would love to stay at the Samaranthan palace for a month, as they did in past visits. Maybe once this was over, if Mother improved, they could return.

After a single jump yesterday afternoon, Uncle Guy had spent time with the western garrison commander, gathering news. Once he sent the siblings through the portal, he and

Aunt Donella would head back to Mintala to give a report to her parents.

They had stayed last night at the garrison. It seemed Uncle Guy needed to replenish his strength before sending them such a long distance. This morning, they had ridden borrowed horses from the garrison to this lonely seaside cliff. Lauryn saw no town nor dwelling.

Uncle Guy spoke quietly to Allyn, no doubt giving him instructions to take care of Lauryn since they glanced her way. Jarell and Xylander seemed to be comparing weapons.

Aunt Donella approached and gave Lauryn a ring on a chain. Lauryn turned the ring around. It was different from the usual Waykeeper rings. Along with the triquetra symbol, a strand of hair wove through it. Lauryn glanced up.

Aunt Donella said, "When you complete your mission, put it on your finger and think of home. Uncle Guy will pull you to him. For years, we never realized that he can act as a portal himself."

She patted Lauryn on the cheek, and went hunting for wildflowers in the grass.

Lauryn put the chain around her neck and tucked it under her collar.

Giada glided up to her. "Are you nervous? I know I would be."

Lauryn swallowed. "Yes. Everything up to this point has been kind of fun. My parents told us what to expect, based on their journey. But I am still anxious about facing the

31

unknown."

"I wish my parents allowed me the freedom you have." Giada's gaze strayed to Allyn. "Your brothers will take care of you."

Lauryn tried to objectively look at her twin to see him as Giada did. He was good looking. He liked to play the big brother role, although she had been born a few minutes before him.

He could read her moods accurately. Like her, he felt their family legacy's heavy responsibility, and tried to live up to it. But unlike her, he covered it up with humor and slight rebelliousness.

"I can take care of myself." Lauryn placed her hand on the dagger belted around her waist. Father and Captain Rodrek had trained her to protect herself. The royal family was a natural target for discontents.

"Are you sure?" Another voice asked from behind them.

Lauryn swung around, placing herself in front of the younger girl, and drawing her weapon.

Xylander stood there frowning. "You're not what I expected." He was tall, yet shorter than Allyn. Which meant she had to look up at him. Being tall herself, she usually had an advantage over others.

She re-sheathed her dagger while raising her chin. "How so?"

"I don't exactly know. Maybe I thought you'd have a halo around your head?"

"What?!" Such an odd thing to say to her.

"Your mother is purported to be the most wise and virtuous person on the three continents." She saw his smirk through the innocent look he gave her.

Arrogant, sneering prince!

"You are the Empress's daughter. As her heir, I thought you would be more...formidable."

Fortunately, Uncle Guy called them or she would've raked him over the coals.

Lauryn marched past Xylander, saying, in Canteoran, the word for "idiot" under her breath.

Giada fell in step beside her. "I think he heard you." She stifled a giggle.

"I hope he did."

Two weather-worn posts stood twelve feet apart. As she drew near, Lauryn could make out the symbols that marked them as wayposts.

Aunt Donella stood up from kneeling. Lauryn saw the square block that she'd uncovered marked a third trinity symbol. Not picking flowers after all.

"The distance is so far, it takes more than one waypost and Waykeeper to travel to another continent." Aunt Donella smiled. Of course, she had done this before during their search for the Isle of Origin. That jump had been disastrous, at least in the short term.

The upside was that during Aunt Donella's and Prince Gensard's enslavement in Canteor, they met Jiana, Giada's mother. And Canteor was converted from paganism. All because of a portal jump gone wrong.

Lauryn's insides churned. Her glance met Xylander's. He looked a little green himself.

"I journeyed by ship from Canteor to Valdeor. This is new to me," he said to her unanswered question.

Uncle Guy had them check to see that their waterskins and satchels were secure. "Line up and hold hands."

Aunt Donella rested her hand on the right waypost. Uncle Guy took the left waypost, grasping hands with Jarell. Jarell stood beside Allyn. Then came Lauryn, who stepped on the buried stone, gripping her twin's hand. Xylander stood beside her on the other side, with Aunt Donella on his right, completing the link.

Lauryn stared at the sharp rocks below, and her stomach protested so much she thought she was going to disgrace herself and throw up.

"Don't look down." She glanced in surprise at Xylander. His eyes showed the same suppressed fear that enveloped her. His hand felt cool and firm. "Keep your eyes on the distance." That was the second time in minutes he read her mind, like Allyn could.

On her other side, Allyn squeezed her hand. She gulped air then breathed in and out like Father taught her before a training session.

Allyn swung his head to look behind him, where Lauryn assumed Giada stood watching.

Mist swirled around their feet and the air vibrated. A hum, which grew louder moment by moment, drowned the sound of the waves hitting the shore far below. A wall of white mist rose before them and slowly in it a distant shore coalesced, as if at the far end of a tunnel.

"Get ready to step forward on my command!" Uncle Guy hollered.

Suddenly, her brother let go of Lauryn's hand. "Allyn!" Lauryn cried, panic rising. A soft, feminine hand grasped hers. Lauryn glimpsed blonde hair moving between her and Allyn before Uncle Guy yelled, "Go!"

Lauryn's eyes glanced down at the waves breaking on the deadly rocks far below as Xylander's hand tugged her forward. She fell toward the churning seas. *It hadn't worked!*

Someone screamed.

Giada's hand slipped from hers. Xylander's iron grip on her right hand pulled her with him. The world around her exploded into black nothingness.

3 Hamleor

Allyn clenched his teeth. He hoped his grasp wasn't crushing Giada's soft hand, but hearing a girl's scream involuntarily made him grip her harder.

The disorientation of not knowing up from down hit him hard. It seemed to last forever. He had never experienced nausea this bad traveling through the portals before. He fought to keep his stomach contents inside. Would it never end?

His breath became ragged as the tunnel vision opened up and the shore came up to meet them. Weightlessness enveloped him, then cold water slammed him hard, breaking his grip on Giada and Jarell.

He plunged beneath the surface, the air knocked out of him. He swiftly kicked his way back into the light. Gulping air, he trod water. Giada's head bobbed up a few feet away. He swam to her and held her up while she gasped for breath.

"Can you swim?" When she nodded yes, he kept pace with her, aware that her dress could drag her down. He didn't worry about Jarell or his sister, who both could swim like fish.

When the sea grew shallow and his feet hit the bottom, Allyn stood. He put an arm around Giada and drew her up on the shore. They both collapsed onto the sand.

"Are you all right?"

Giada mumbled yes and brushed wet hair from her face.

Glancing around, Allyn saw Jarell on all fours coughing further down the beach. Turning his head the other way he only saw the empty beach. Jumping to his feet, he shaded his eyes and searched the sea for Lauryn. The Canteor prince could look after himself.

"Lauryn let go of me. Or I of her." Giada stood up beside him, wearing a concerned expression. She clutched her hands, face pale.

Jarell came jogging over. "Where are Lauryn and Xylander?" He seemed to notice Giada for the first time. "What are you doing here?" Surprise and anger chased across his features. "I thought your parents only let you come to say goodbye. We don't need a pampered princess to keep track of."

"Jarell, calm yourself." Gazing at Giada in consternation, Allyn gently asked, "Why did you come, Giada?"

Giada's lower lip trembled. Then she squared her shoulders. "I wanted to be a part of your adventure. Nothing exciting ever comes my way."

"Your parents might seem overprotective. But this trip is more dangerous than you realize." Although Allyn wanted

37

to spend more time in her company—*when had she grown so lovely?*—he doubted she was up to this expedition's challenges.

Had his smile accidently convinced her to come along? If so, he was responsible if anything happened to her.

"If Lauryn came, why couldn't I?" She had a stubborn expression that he knew from childhood. Usually docile until she really wanted something, Giada could dig her heels in.

"Lauryn trains with Father," Jarell was quick to point out. "She can defend herself. You live surrounded by guards, the court's darling. And I, for one, don't want to babysit you."

In answer, Giada pulled out a small jeweled dagger from her pocket. It looked more like a toy than a weapon. "I brought a weapon."

Jarell snorted. Allyn poked him in the ribs before his brother could humiliate her.

Putting on his patient, big brother voice, Allyn crossed his arms. "You aren't prepared for this. You don't know how to fight. Have you ever used that thing?"

She replaced her knife in her pocket. Then she put her hands on her hips in a scolding attitude, which was ruined by her dripping-wet kitten appearance. "Your mother was no warrior. Yet at a similar age to me, she went on a quest with your father in a much more dangerous time period. We live in a time of peace. Are you saying you and your brother couldn't protect me? You carry your father's sword."

Allyn had hoped no one would notice the Crestin sword

in the old, scuffed scabbard he had placed it in.

She was partially right about his mother. *Confound it!*

"I guess the point is moot, now that you are here." Allyn shook his head. "It's not like we can send you back." *Yet.*

"Just try to keep up." Allyn picked up his satchel and slung it over his back.

"Yes, Your Highness." Giada sounded cowed.

Allyn couldn't have that.

"Call me Allyn. No need for formality. Unless you'd prefer me to refer to you as Your Highness, Princess of Samarantha?" He raised an eyebrow. She relaxed at his teasing tone.

They had traveled far enough west that the sun had recently peeked over the horizon here.

Being the oldest, he took charge. He had planned on letting Lauryn lead, but since their separation, it fell upon his shoulders to guide the other two. Once they met up with Lauryn, he'd hand over the reins.

He relished the adventure, not the prize. If being saddled with a kingdom could be called a prize. More like a responsibility. One Lauryn wanted. She could have it.

Finding a break in the dunes, Allyn headed inland, knowing his brother would bring up the rear. He marched ahead on a well-worn path leading from the shore. He kept a pace that Giada could keep up with, figuring her wet riding habit would slow her down until it dried in the sun.

After walking an hour, they came to a fishing village. A

few cottages were scattered about an inlet. Small boats bobbed at sea.

He used some of his coins to buy hot bread at the local tavern. He sent Jarell to discover their location.

Jarell soon came back. He had learned the way to Losen Harbor. Waiting until they passed beyond the village, Allyn pulled out the map rolled in a waterproof skin from his satchel and they traced their journey.

"The fisherwoman said it is two day's journey to Oster, the largest city."

"All right. We can buy supplies and horses there."

They slept in a barn at an abandoned homestead that night. Then in the open air the next.

In the early hours, before taking to the road each day, Allyn showed Giada how to use his dagger. He sparred with Jarell, then walked her through the simpler moves. In a real fight, he planned on protecting her himself, but in unforeseen circumstances, he wanted her to be able to defend herself if they became separated.

She was as awkward as a toddler learning to walk, but at least she made an effort. She seemed determined to fit in and not be a burden. He admired her for that.

The third day they took a ferry over the River Ost and came to the city of Oster. The seaport capital sprawled along a curved harbor. Wooden houses, painted white or gray, with slate roofs, stood in neat rows. Flags provided color. From his studies, Allyn knew the townspeople had divided it into quarters, and each quarter flew their ruling family's pennant.

"Change of plans," Allyn said as they waited among a crowd of merchants and travelers to enter the gate. "A ship would be a faster way to get to Losen Harbor. There we can rent horses to take us into the mountains. We have to assume Lauryn and Xylander will also follow in Father's steps. That's the most logical way that we'll meet up."

"I'll look into it." Jarell sounded eager. He loved ships.

He pulled Allyn aside and said in a low tone, "Should I get passage for the princess on the next ship to Samarantha? She's going to be an anchor around our necks."

"I've been thinking the same thing. That is, about sending her home." Allyn made sure she wasn't able to hear them, caught up as she was watching the crowds. "Find out what ships are available."

The three strode together toward the harbor. When they were nearly there, the street opened onto a square, central market. It boasted wares from around the kingdoms. Here they split up.

"Meet at the cathedral," Allyn commanded. The spire towered above the city, easy to see.

Jarell headed to the wharf.

"Stick close to me." Allyn glanced down at Giada. "Pickpockets abound in places like this."

"I know." She gave him the 'I'm not a baby anymore'

look, the same as Allyria would. "We have them in Samarantha too, you know."

"But guards surround you there. If anyone recognizes you here, they could kidnap you for ransom." He had to get it across to her that this wasn't home.

Giada lost her superior smile, her usual timid expression replacing it, as she glanced around. She moved a step closer to him.

Allyn sighed inwardly. He wasn't trying to be mean. He wanted her to be alert to the dangers.

The smell of baked bread and smoked meats competed with many animals' odors.

It seemed they had come on the day of the sheep auction. The animals bleated everywhere—some cream-colored, many of variegated shades of brown, others with black faces. Some shepherds used crooks to guide their flock through the crowd, and others used dogs.

Allyn steered them through the throngs of people and animals to the merchant booths. They ate hot lamb chunks on a stick. He bought Giada a satchel, a blanket and a waterskin.

A carriage bearing a ruling families' crest on the door rolled up. The crowd respectfully moved away from it. Allyn watched as a lovely girl disembarked, followed by her servant and guards. He recalled which family she belonged to, having had to memorize the ruling family trees of all the lands.

The gravity of his situation pressed on him. If he became

high king, he might have to make a marriage alliance with someone like her. He wasn't sure he was ready for the responsibilities that came with the crown.

His parents seemed invincible. He couldn't quite believe Mother might die. Soon. And Lauryn had always been the next in line, not him.

Without paying attention to where they were going, he led them into an alleyway. Music and movement drew his eye at the far end.

A swish of air beside him gave him warning. He spun around; his senses sharp. A big man leapt at him from behind a pile of crates, blade drawn.

Allyn drew the Crestin sword and blocked the blow.

Giada had been beside him a moment ago. He cried out for her to stay behind him.

He fought the assailant, sure of victory, since the man's attack lacked any skill. It was easy to predict his blunt moves. The thug tried to back Allyn against the wall, so Allyn kept moving toward the far end of the alley and safety.

"Allyn! Another one," Giada cried.

Quickly glancing behind him, Allyn had an impression of Giada huddling in an empty doorway halfway down the alley. But his concentration was on the second foe who strode toward them, a short sword in his hand.

Turning back to the first man, Allyn made a move Father had taught him and sent the thug's blade flying. Using his hilt, he hit the assailant in the temple and the big man fell.

Spinning, he changed direction and threw himself at the second attacker, who reached for Giada. The man grabbed Giada above the elbow. Allyn slashed at the man's outstretched arm, causing him to yell with pain and loosen his hold on her. Allyn blocked the aggressor's sword, then kicked him in the gut. The attacker dropped to the ground, moaning.

Allyn grabbed Giada's hand and raced out of the alleyway into the swirling crowd of people.

Allyn put his hands on Giada's shoulders. "Did he hurt you?" Anger welled up at the thought of the brute harming her. Allyn should have been paying attention!

"I'm all right." Her lower lip trembled. Then she leaned into his chest. Her shaking let him know she was crying, as did the damp seeping into his shirt. Allyn put his arm around her, like he would for Lauryn or Allyria. "Shh. You are safe now. It's going to be all right." He soothed her the way he would his sisters. But she wasn't his sister, and he didn't feel brotherly holding her.

After another minute, she pulled back and wiped her eyes. "You and Jarell were right. I shouldn't have come."

"You are here now. We'll work on some defensive moves without weapons." He put Giada's arm through his.

Allyn purchased a respectable dagger for her. He also bought boys clothes, a cap, and a kerchief.

"Let's find my brother. He's probably done by now."

They met Jarell in the cathedral's portico.

Having a few hours before the tide turned, Giada slipped inside to light a candle and pray. Allyn followed and knelt in a pew and prayed for the strength to be the leader they needed.

Jarell paced, too restless to stay in one place. He visited the different shrines around the cathedral's perimeter.

Finishing his prayers, Allyn joined Jarell in a side chapel.

"I looked for a ship to Samarantha." Jarell crossed his arms, his face set. "Unfortunately, the next one won't depart for nearly a week."

Allyn sighed. "I don't see a way to send Giada back without delaying our trip further."

"She doesn't belong traveling with us," Jarell hissed. "What are her parents going to say?"

"We can't leave her behind, either. I'll take the blame no matter what happens."

Rubbing the back of his neck, Allyn said, "The One that Fashioned All allowed her to join us. The supernatural portal guardian wouldn't have let her pass unless it was so."

His gaze fell on her, as she wandered the aisles. "She may have a part to play." But the responsibility for her safety weighed heavily on him, especially after the incident in the market.

Leaving Jarell, he found a small room in an out-of-the-way nook. Allyn got Giada's attention and motioned her over. When she joined him, he took the boy's clothes from the satchel. "It's best if you change, Giada. A boy attracts less unwanted attention."

She glanced at him and blushed. Without a word, she hurried into the closet. She returned in a short time. He had guessed her size well. He refused to stare at her.

She removed the jeweled pins from her hair, releasing her long, golden braid. "Please, will you cut my hair?"

Allyn stared at the long tresses, then met her eyes with their determined expression. He removed the Crestin sword from his scabbard. Her eyes went wide as he held it to the nape of her neck.

"The sword's blade is fine enough to shear hair. My dagger would only butcher it."

When she nodded, jaw tense, he grabbed a fistful of her hair. It was as soft as he imagined. He was close enough to see the regret in her eyes as he hacked it off with a couple of swipes.

Although dressed as a boy, she would still draw attention. Her short hair was a riot of curls around her girlish face.

"Do I look like a boy?" she whispered.

Sort of. Except for those brilliant green eyes and long eyelashes. And the fact that she looked like the illustration of a pixie in one of Allyria's books. He swallowed. He couldn't say that. "Put the cap on."

He handed her the knit hat. She stretched it over her blonde curls and adjusted it. "Does it help?"

"Much better."

Jarell joined them. He took one look at her and removed his vest. "You can borrow this till Allyn buys you another." When they both looked askance at him, he pursed his lips. "It has multiple pockets with things I brought specifically for this trip."

Knowing Jarell's penchant for experiments, Giada looked wary as she put it on. It further disguised her shapely form.

They headed back outside.

Watching her critically, Jarell frowned. "You need to walk like a boy. Swagger. Don't mince your steps."

Allyn hoped she wouldn't regret her rash decision to come along.

Once on board the *Venture*, Allyn was pleased when he realized it was a Valdeoran merchant ship. The captain showed them deference upon learning who they were.

Giada slept in the captain's cabin, while he moved in with his second-in-command. Allyn and Jarell opted to sleep on deck rather than the hammocks below.

What would've taken two weeks on horseback would take only four days by ship.

Allyn decided to pass the time by continuing to work on Giada's defensive skills. He took turns with Jarell teaching her how to use her new dagger.

His gut clenched every time he thought about how close she had come to being hurt. His fault. He should've been watching where they were going rather than thinking about the noble girl.

Giada's eyes had shadows under them, as if she were haunted by her near escape. Maybe because of it, she threw her heart into the lessons on defending herself.

On the third day out, Allyn approached her when she came above deck.

"Today I'd like to work on defensive moves that don't include weapons. The assailants you'll encounter will be bigger and stronger than you."

She nodded her agreement, fear in the back of her eyes.

"But you have some advantages. Surprise, your smaller size and quick movements. Remember, what I teach you is how to escape an assailant. Not to prolong a fight. You will lose if you do. Once you are free of your attacker, run away! Do you understand?"

"Yes. I know you aren't training me to be a warrior. That would take years." Giada stood straighter.

"These are the techniques my father taught my sisters." He gave her an encouraging smile.

Her expression perked up. "You mean Allyria knows how to defend herself? She is younger and smaller than I."

"Yes. She can be quite fierce." He chuckled and got Giada to grin.

"You must use your elbows to hit an opponent standing

behind you. And kick his shins. Spread your fingers. They can be used to poke at his eyes. Don't be squeamish. Always remember, it's your life or his."

She swallowed, but nodded.

He walked her through some moves. "Also, when someone grabs you, let your body go limp. Slip out of his grasp, knee him in an area to cause maximum pain. And your greatest asset? Run. Avoid an encounter if possible. Let Jarell and me deal with it, like your guards normally would."

"I remember my personal guard telling me to keep alert and trust my instincts. If something felt off, listen to that inner voice."

"Exactly."

Allyn decided he didn't want to embarrass Giada with an audience. He took her hand and led her to the ship's stern, away from prying eyes.

"Do you trust me? Really trust me?" He gazed into her eyes.

They widened at his question. "I've known you my whole life, Your High—, uh, Allyn." She flushed, suddenly shy. "Yes, I do."

"Good. You are going to use everything I taught you to escape. Well, all but that last move." They both blushed as she realized what he meant.

Before she could turn chicken, he spun and grabbed her from behind. He held her hard enough that she couldn't wiggle loose, but not hard enough to hurt her.

She stiffened for a heartbeat, then she elbowed him and kicked backward. The move was ineffective, since his feet were braced apart. She paused, but didn't give up. Tipping her head back, she smacked him in the chin. Suddenly, she dropped, squirming out of his hold. She landed a kick to his shin that caused him to stifle a groan.

He suffered the bruises with manly fortitude. He was willing to suffer worse if it kept her safe.

He perceived Jarell leaning against the bulwark, smirking at his pain. With a flick of his eyebrows he signaled his brother. Jarell moved stealthily behind Giada. Unaware of his approach, she blushed and rubbed her hands down her trousers.

"Not bad. Are you ready to do it again?" Allyn asked.

Shaking slightly, she jutted her chin out with determination. "Yes." Her gaze remained steadily on him, watching for his first move.

She screamed as Jarell grabbed her around her neck and put a hand over her mouth. Fear filled her face. Her heel caught Jarell's shin but he held tight. She bit his hand, once, then harder, before he finally let go.

She spun around to see who attacked her while she backed away from them both, freeing her dagger from its scabbard.

"Wow! I had no idea you could be such a wildcat." Jarell nursed his hand, with bloody marks.

Panting, she glanced between the brothers. She glared

at Allyn. "Not fair!"

Even though it was hard to do, Allyn wiped away any trace of compassion as he stared back at her. "No one will fight you fairly, princess. As a pretty girl, you will attract attention. As royals, we are always targets. Your life may depend on your skills alone, until you are home and back under constant guard. Until then, you must learn to be vigilant."

She huffed and stormed away.

Guilt clawed at him. He soon caught up to her. He grabbed her wrist and gently swung her around. "Giada," he breathed, "I have to make sure you are safe. If anything happened to you..." He swallowed.

Tears glistened in her eyes. She stood stiffly for a minute, then her shoulders sagged. "I know." In a softer voice, she added, "I still trust you."

A hard knot in his chest loosened. "Allyria and Lauryn would be proud of you."

"Do you think so?" She brushed her hand across her eyes, her voice hopeful. "I hope we meet up with your sister at Losen Harbor. Do you think she'll be there?"

"I'm planning on it. My twin sense says yes."

4 Nyrmidion Isles

The tunnel in the mist grew bigger and bigger. The land came up to meet Lauryn. She hit the ground, then rolled from the impact as her father had taught her. Ending up on her back, the breath knocked from her, she stared at the blue sky. The sun wasn't where she expected.

With a groan, she rolled over to see Xylander sprawled nearby.

Checking herself over, and finding only a few bruises, she stood.

They'd landed in a clearing. Oak trees of great height formed a tight ring around them. In the center, a monolithic stone lay on its side, rust colored stains discoloring it. It had a giant crack which split it in two, as if someone had taken a great hammer to it. It took a moment for Lauryn to realize this place's significance. An altar for sacrifice. Chills sped up and down Lauryn's spine.

In the still air, not a bird trilled.

She saw no signs of her brothers or Giada, whom she assumed joined them the last moment. She took a few steps toward the thick brush and nearly toppled over as she tripped on something in the weeds.

A strong hand gripped her and prevented her from falling. "We seem to be the only two who made it." Xylander had joined her.

Glancing down, Lauryn saw the trinity symbol on the buried stone. She had almost fallen over the waypost that drew them here.

Lauryn stepped away and Xylander released her. Her heart stilled as she replayed their last moments. "Giada dropped my hand when we jumped through."

"Giada? But she wasn't supposed to come with us." Shock made him rigid.

"She slipped between me and Allyn at the last moment."

"What?! That is unlike her." A frown creased his brow. "She would never defy her parents that way. Your brother must have grabbed her and dragged her through."

Although she thought it highly unlikely, Lauryn didn't refute him out loud. She recalled Allyn looking back at Giada before they jumped. She supposed he could have reached for her.

"Something she said made me feel she wished she could come with us. I wonder—"

"She would never do such a thing." Xylander's face darkened. "Your brother had better take care of my betrothed, or I will kill him."

It was Lauryn's turn to be surprised. "Betrothed? Giada never wrote me about it in her recent letters."

Xylander looked embarrassed. "Not officially betrothed. But that was the motive for my visit. I hope to gain her father's permission."

Neither Xylander nor Giada had shown any affection, or even interest in each other, during the preceding days' interactions. Lauryn thought it an odd way to conduct a romance. But arranged marriages among nobles was normal.

Lauryn even might have to marry as part of an alliance to strengthen ties between Valdeoran provinces, or even her country and another.

She had no attachments, which would make it easier, she supposed, to learn to love the man she married one day. Well, except for...

Xylander interrupted her thoughts. "Unlike Valdeoran women, Uncle Gensard has raised her to be very biddable." Xylander smirked. "She'll make me an admirable wife."

Lauryn's ire rose at his words. She pitied Giada if that was the only reason Xylander chose to betroth himself to her.

Deciding further conversation with him on this topic was useless, she picked up her satchel and waterskin from where they landed after her fall. "Well, I guess we should find out where we are. I have never visited Hamleor. Have you?"

"No, I haven't." He hefted his belongings. "I'll lead." Without checking to see if she followed, he strode away on the only path leading from the ring of sacred trees.

Her frustration barely in check, Lauryn stomped behind

him. She outranked him. Yet in order to pass him, she'd have to run ahead of him. She refused to sully her dignity. She clenched her teeth. When they got to civilization, she'd show him that she was meant to lead the group. *After all, it was her quest, not his! Stubborn prince.*

When he finally noticed how she struggled to keep up with his longer strides, he perceptibly slowed down. *Was that a glance of regret he sent her?* But he made no apology.

After an hour, they ran across a wider road. They stopped for a drink. Xylander turned left.

"Why that way?" She nearly went the other way to spite him. Time to assert herself. But as much as she wanted to defy him, acting childish would accomplish nothing. Acting diplomatically showed her leadership qualities.

"Why not?"

He had a point. Although she made sure to stride ahead of him.

In a short while, they came upon a village. It had an odd look about it. At one house, someone had fashioned a ship's hatch into a door. Another dwelling had portholes for windows. A broken ship's mast held up a clothesline's end. Urging his donkey to move, a man wearing a horned helmet plowed a vegetable garden.

Lauryn stopped, gazing around.

Xylander turned to glance at her. "What is it?"

"I know this place. We are in the Nyrmidion Islands!"

"The pirate's lair?" Xylander put a hand on his sword

55

hilt, his jaw tight, glancing about.

A few children playing in a yard spotted them. Eyes curious, they jumped to their feet and ran down the road to a larger dwelling.

Within moments, a young man came out and headed toward them. Tall and well-muscled, his dark glance roamed over them. Brown hair brushed his shoulders. He wore a short sword belted over his leather tunic.

The children hung back, but several adults seeing him, dropped what they were doing and followed in his wake.

"Stay behind me." Xylander drew his sword and held it at the ready.

Ignoring him, Lauryn walked past Xylander. "Irdek! May the winds always favor you." She used the ritual Nyrmidion greeting.

"And may the waves ever carry you to safety. Well met, Lauryn. What brings you here?" He glanced down the road behind her as if searching for the rest of her family.

"That's a long tale." She gestured to the baffled Xylander. "For now I travel with Crown Prince Xylander of Canteor."

"I am honored by two royals visiting my kingdom. Please, let us show our hospitality while I hear your tale."

Irdek led them to the largest dwelling in the village from which he had come.

Xylander had put away his sword, but still fondled the hilt, his body tense. He asked Lauryn under his breath, "How do you know these people? Aren't they the dreaded pirates of the Stormy Seas?"

"It helps to be the Empress's daughter." She smugly grinned at him. "We have treaties with all the lands."

He grunted as they entered.

Inside the wooden building were tables and chairs made from ships' planks. Rich carpets lay on the wood floor. A gray-haired woman stood at the fireplace, stirring a pot. A kettle hung above the flames. A younger woman chopped meat. Through an open door, Lauryn glimpsed another room beyond with cushions on the floor, where an old man sat.

"Mother, look who has come to visit. Princess Lauryn and her traveling companion, Canteor's prince." Then, Irdek faced away as he spoke with a man who appeared in the doorway.

"Highness," Irda smiled shyly. "You remind me of your mother at that age. Is she well?" She held a spoon in one hand and reached for clay mugs on a shelf above her with the other. Passing the spoon to the young woman, Irda poured two mugs of strong tea. She placed them on the rough table and gestured for them to sit.

Lauryn thanked her and sat. Xylander declined and remained standing with his arms crossed behind her chair, as if he were her bodyguard.

She spoke of her mother's poor health.

Lauryn hissed as Irda headed into the back room, "Xylander, you're making a bad impression. This is time for diplomacy. You did learn that as crown prince, or don't they teach it in your country?"

Her words had their intended effect.

"I'm not a savage." He thumped into the chair next to her, but ignored the drink. "They are." But he said it in an undertone. "Don't you know how dangerous a position we are in? They show no mercy to outsiders."

"My mother saved Irdek's life when he was a child. They would never harm her daughter. It would be against their code of honor. And since you are my companion, you fall under the same protection." She glared at him. "That is if you can keep your temper and show no fear."

At his glance of shocked insult, she knew he would toe the line. Her brothers hated to be accused of cowardice, and from what she had seen of Xylander, he reacted the same way.

They suspended further whispered conversation when Irdek joined them. Behind him, several village elders slipped into the house. Irda brought in the old man from the other room.

He wore a helmet with two reddened horns, a leather vest, and mismatched metal arm bracers. The old woman led him by the hand. Lauryn saw the gray glint coating his eyes. The once great Nyrmidion leader was blind.

Although he couldn't see her, Lauryn stood when they stopped at the table. "Hail, Marjek Red Horns from the Reina's ambassador."

"Hail, Princess Lauryn. You and your guest are welcome in my home." He stood tall and muscular, still formidable, even now.

A chair scraped against the floor as Xylander stood. "Hail from Princess Sefira of Canteor to Marjek Red Horns. I am her son Xylander. My father is Prince Leander of Samarantha. Prosperity to you and yours for your gracious hospitality." He crossed his fists over his chest in the old way of saluting a king.

Xylander impressed Lauryn with his greeting. And by the quirk of his lips, he knew it.

Irda settled Marjek at the table. A white-haired villager joined them and Irdek introduced him as Dahl, an honored elder.

As they sat, Marjek stared over their heads. "What brings you so far from home, daughter of Valdeor?"

"The Reina and my father have sent my brother and me on a quest to prove our worthiness. This is the first stop on my journey." *Whether I meant it to be or not.*

"What is this quest?" Irdek glanced from one to the other, curiosity and a quick flash of greed crossing his expression.

"To find a bird. A very rare bird called a firebird or a phoenix. It's very large and purplish red in color. It nests in the mountains." Lauryn was relieved to see Irdek's interest wane. She didn't need the Nyrmidions getting involved in seeking her treasure.

"Ah. For a feast. We have the great wingless bird, the nuknuk, on the islands. It weighs as much as a man. We kill and eat it for certain feasts."

Xylander's expression was one of barely disguised disdain. "The phoenix's feather is supposed to be magical. The potentate of my country wears it in his turban for a prosperous reign." Xylander gestured at the horned helmet of their host. "Similar to your people's leader wearing the gray mammoth horns."

Irdek nodded in understanding. "Then you eat it."

Xylander rolled his eyes and didn't respond.

Before the two young men could talk at cross purposes any more, Lauryn interjected, "My brother Allyn and I are competing to find it first." She left off the part about the quest's reward, the throne. Even here, they accepted that she was meant to don the Reina's mantle as firstborn, though their form of government was a patriarchy. Losing face in front of the Nyrmidions wouldn't give her an advantage if she wanted their help.

"In your people's many travels," she wouldn't say 'raids', "have you come across mention of it?"

Irdek gave her a sympathetic look. "Now I understand why you have come to us. But I'm sorry to say, we don't have your firebird in our islands." He glanced at the elder, Dahl, who shook his head no.

He turned to Marjek, his father. "I've never heard of it." Marjek spread his hands open. "But you are welcome to our hospitality until you depart."

Dahl had a sour expression at those words. Catching her gaze, he shuttered his face. The elders left soon after.

Watching them go, Lauryn wondered if the elders missed the olden days of pirating. Not all Nyrmidions embraced the changes her mother had wrought to their culture during her stay here.

Lauryn shared news of her family with Irdek, Marjek and Irda. Xylander sat stoically listening. She sipped the bitter tea, putting it down when a commotion erupted outside.

Dahl stepped halfway through the door and motioned to Irdek. "We've taken a foreign prisoner." Heart leaping at the thought that it might be her brothers, Lauryn and Xylander followed Irdek to the doorway.

Eight warriors surrounded a young man with dusky brown hair and broad shoulders, who stood half a head above them. He had a cut on his cheek, but the warrior beside him sported a black eye. They had tied the prisoner's arms behind his back and led him with a noose around his neck.

The elders and villagers crowded behind them.

"We caught this foreigner at the altar of sacrifice." Dahl spat at the sacrilege.

As the procession stopped at the chief's home, the captive glanced up. Relief, followed by humor, flashed across his face as his glance caught her eyes.

"Will you please call off your sea-wolves, Lauryn? I meant to join you earlier but I was delayed."

Lauryn's eyes widened as she recognized him.

"Any friend of the Reina's daughter is welcome in my home." Marjek Red Horns stood directly behind Lauryn. He might be unable to see, but he was quick to listen and act.

Hiding her emotions behind her court mask, Lauryn turned toward the elder man. "Thank you for interceding, Marjek. I am indebted to you."

Within moments, the prisoner was freed and soon they were all seated around the table.

Frowning, Lauryn faced the unexpected arrival. The more she thought about it, the more she was sure her father had sent him to watch over her. "Please enlighten us as to your presence." She raised an eyebrow at him.

His eyes twinkled at her discomfort in his otherwise somber face. He turned to the others gathered there. "I am Prince Everard II of Winterhome. The Reina's consort requested my participation in the twin's quest as mentor and guard." He glanced at her from the side of his eye, to see her reaction.

Lauryn clenched her hands under the table. Even though he had personally trained her in combat, Father still thought she needed a nursemaid. Everard was conscientious, staid, and unflappable in most situations. Even a short while ago, he had shown no panic at the very real possibility of the Nyrmidions stringing him up. Of course, he was a swordsman of great renown, and someone she wanted at her side in battle. Her father chose well, though she would never admit it. But Everard tended to act superior because he was twenty years to her almost eighteen.

"I thought this exercise was to prove myself." Lauryn bit out the words. Everard might be Allyn's best friend, but now that they were separated, Ever was here to babysit her. *Ugh!*

"Ah, but you must survive in order to win. You are amongst friends now, but you won't always be." Although she didn't want him here, Everard was sensitive to the situation. Of course, he would be. He prided himself on his diplomacy. Another annoying trait.

After sharing a meal of stew with them, Irda showed the young men a ladder that led to a loft where they could store their things and sleep that night. Irdek gave Lauryn his room.

Stating her intention to stretch her legs before turning in, Lauryn escaped outside, her companions following. They strolled through town, ignoring the inhabitants' wary glances.

"Well, that was a waste of time. I have no idea why your friend Guy would send us here," Xylander complained. "These savages cannot help us."

"I didn't catch your name." Everard raised an eyebrow at the younger man. "Prince Alloryn didn't mention you in his correspondence to me."

Lauryn made the introductions, then answered Xylander. "Uncle Guy didn't mean to send us here."

Turning to Everard she explained. "Hearing of our journey, Xylander wished to join us. We were headed for the Lost Mountains of Hamleor. We got separated when we jumped through the portal. Hopefully Allyn and Jarell made it with Giada."

"I wondered where your brothers were." Everard frowned. "You shouldn't travel alone."

"She's not alone. She has me." Xylander puffed out his chest and patted his scimitar. "My father was the champion gladiator for a dozen years. I inherited his prowess. I can defend her."

Everard didn't look impressed.

She told Everard more detail than she shared with the Nyrmidions. She hoped changing the subject would diffuse the manly rivalry going on between the two young men.

Xylander stalked ahead when she mentioned Giada's sudden addition.

"So your brothers are most likely in Hamleor." Everard ran his hand through his hair, mussing it up. His placid calm must truly be ruffled. "I would have been here sooner, but Great-Grandmama died last week. She was 101 years old."

"Oh, Everard, I'm so sorry." Lauryn remembered the feisty old woman. She laid a hand on his arm.

"Why is that hot-headed bantam rooster along on this

venture?" Everard kept his voice low, frowning as he watched the younger prince swagger. Only someone as tall as Everard's six-foot two frame would consider Xylander's nearly six feet as small.

"To be honest, I don't know. Aunt Donella insisted he come."

"Your father trusts me to protect you." He spoke with self-assurance, yet no puffed-up pride. Yet his voice held a note of jealousy. "The Canteoran prince seems superfluous."

"Like you?" She rolled her eyes. "I don't need either of you. I can take care of myself."

Instead of being insulted, Everard laughed. "Is that so?" He sobered. "Do you really prefer him to me? He's a bit young and brash."

Lauryn didn't share her opinion of either of them with Everard. When much younger, she had had a crush on Ever. His handsome face. His broad shoulders. His hazel eyes that teased her. As children they spent time every summer in Winterhome's cooler climate. She had tagged along after Allyn and Everard every chance she got.

But in the last few years he had become bossy. And she was, after all, the Reina's heir. At least, she was until a few days ago. She outranked Everard, but he never let that stop him from chastising her when he decided she needed it. Much too often for her liking.

She suddenly realized that Everard had asked her a question while she was woolgathering. She hoped he didn't notice her embarrassment. "What did you say?"

"I asked if Guy gave you a ring to activate the portals."

"Yes, but I'm only supposed to use it to return home." She pulled it out from under her tunic where it hung on a chain. "It's not the usual ring. It has a strand of Uncle Guy's hair wrapped around it. When I put it on, he will know it and pull me toward him."

Everard drew close and examined it.

Lauryn could smell his leather and citrus scent. Suddenly painfully aware of him, heat spread up her face.

Everard seemed oblivious of her attraction to him. *As always.* She was doomed forever to only be his best friend's sister.

"I've wondered if he could act as a portal himself, marked with the interlocking ovals birthmark." He dropped the ring and stepped away.

Lauryn could breathe easily again.

After talking it over further, they decided the best option was to board a ship to Losen Harbor, the nearest town to the Lost Mountains.

In the more than twenty years since Mother had stayed in the isles, the town had built a jetty. They had no natural harbors due to the rocky formations near the shore that caused shipwrecks. Shipwrecks that they had taken advantage of, and even caused in the past. The trading ships used the jetty since Mother's treaty with Marjek. Although a few other islands in the chains still followed the pirating ways, the islands under Marjek's rule no longer did.

Two weeks passed while they waited for a scheduled vessel sailing from Valdeor to Hamleor.

The three used the time to keep in shape. They ran for an hour every morning, followed by sparring matches with their swords. Lauryn was used to Everard beating her in their match although she put up a good fight.

Xylander surprised her. He wasn't boasting when he said he learned from the best. He seemed evenly matched with Everard. She wondered how he would fare against her brother, the only swordsman in the realm that could beat Everard, occasionally. Well, except Father, who could trounce them both.

Several village warriors had taken to watching them spar in the cool hour after dawn.

"Where did you learn to fight, again?" Everard wiped his forehead after a particularly grueling match.

"My father is a mighty warrior. Although he was born in Samarantha, he eventually ended up across the sea in Canteor. Every year on King Pashmi's birthday, he, the great ruler, held a gladiator contest. My father won for twelve years in a row."

"How did a slave marry Princess Sefira?" Everard sounded skeptical.

"He wasn't born a slave." Xylander's jaw clenched, his

eyes haughty. "My father is Prince Leander, oldest son of Samarantha's former king. He and my grandfather, King Xander, had a falling out. King Xander banished him and made his second son, Prince Gensard, his heir.

"For his mastery in the gladiator ring, King Pashmi assigned my father as bodyguard to my mother. They fell in love and married. My father taught me everything he knew."

Whether because of the story or because they wished to try their hand at besting him, the village warriors challenged Xylander to hand-to-hand combats every morning after that. The Nyrmidions had a reputation as fierce warriors throughout all the lands. Few villages had survived their raiding bands in the time when they terrorized the neighboring countries.

That allowed an opportunity for Lauryn to be alone with Everard.

Lauryn had to admit she enjoyed Everard's companionship. Whether practicing with the sword, or discussing their plans, he was almost as good as having Allyn at her side. But she'd never tell him that.

Although, if Allyn were here, Everard would spend all his time with her brother. The thought that she was second best in his eyes depressed her.

Three weeks after they arrived, when she and the two young men returned from their run, they heard cries as they approached the village. Looking down from the hilltop, they saw men clashing swords in the street. Women, and even children, stood in their doorways with weapons or farm implements, ready to protect their houses.

Marauders!

Lauryn drew her dagger, but before she could move, Everard grabbed her arm and Xylander moved between her and the pitched battle.

"What are you doing? We have to help them!" she sputtered as she tried to free herself.

"Think, Lauryn! You are the heir of the realm." Determination mixed with regret filled Everard's gaze. "I know they are your friends, but they are Nyrmidion warriors, not helpless peasants. They can take care of themselves."

She glanced back at the fighting, catching sight of Irdek in the middle of the conflict, slaying the invading force. The villagers rallied around him.

Everard dragged her back the way they had come.

"But they have shown us hospitality!" Lauryn argued. "Your swords could make a difference."

She glanced at Xylander, poised with his scimitar, every line of his body screaming with a desire to fight. She could tell that he at least agreed with her.

"You are both heirs to your kingdoms. You have a duty to your subjects first." Everard stood firm.

"You speak of duty. But what honor is there in not defending a sworn ally. Our treaty guarantees Valdeor's help. It certainly appears to me that another tribe has come to take Marjek's leadership from him. As the only Valdeorans able to help, is it honorable to stand by and watch?"

Lauryn knew she had won the argument when Everard huffed and loosened his grip. "You are going to be the death of me, Lauryn."

She smirked.

Everard hissed, "Stay close to me or I will carry you out of the fight over my shoulder if necessary." He was capable of doing it, too.

Approaching from the rear, the two young men attacked, as Lauryn hung back. Not that she was afraid, exactly. No. She had never killed, and the thought of purposely wounding another person sickened her. Her father trained her in self-defense, not combat.

Meanwhile, Everard and Xylander each made quick work of a marauder.

But seeing the children so brave, defending their homes and lives, she determined to do her best. The fighting had moved away from her toward the town center. She headed that way, seeking to fight alongside her companions.

A sound behind her gave her a second's warning of danger. A meaty hand clamped over her mouth, and a strong arm grasped her around the middle. She froze for a second, then kicked and squirmed. He oomphed as her boot caught him in the shin, but he didn't let go.

Her captor dragged her off the road. Lifting her up he went down the cliff's path toward the beach.

A boat rested near the shore. Four men were poised to

set off when they reached it. One of them passed a rope around her wrists. Her captor dropped her unceremoniously in the boat's bottom.

She cried out, but the village was too far away for anyone to hear her over the sound of the waves and fighting.

By the time she sat up, the men had pushed the boat into the sea and took up their oars.

They dressed like islanders. A rival tribe?

"Where are you taking me?" She stared at the bulky man who had carried her. He must be close to seven feet tall. She swallowed; her mouth dry.

"No questions." He leered at her and she huddled in the bottom of the boat, reviewing her options. If she could jump overboard and try to swim, her tied hands would hamper her. She could reveal her identity and offer herself for ransom. Or she could keep silent and watch for an opportunity to escape. She decided on the last option until she knew more.

Looking back, she thought she saw someone on the cliff staring at the boat, before they disappeared.

5 Avalanche

*W*e've already waited three days, Allyn." Jarell frowned and pushed away his empty trencher. "I don't think Lauryn is coming. She must have followed her own path."

Tankards clinked, tavern patrons conversed, and music from a hand organ swirled around the room. Pipe tobacco's sweet scent mingled with the savory smell of roasting meat, as Allyn contemplated their next move.

Three days of waiting in Losen Harbor meant that they were all on edge.

Allyn sighed, absently pushing around meat gristle with his fork. Jarell was right.

Not that he liked leaving the foreign prince as his sister's sole protector. Xylander, for all his arrogance, was the son of the most decorated gladiator of all time in Canteor. The scimitar he carried wasn't only for show. But Allyn worried about his character and motives.

Only a few days ago, Allyn's twin sense had tingled with danger for Lauryn. But now his twin feeling was lessening in intensity.

He must accept that he could do nothing to help her.

He looked up. Jarell leaned forward, impatience written on his face. Giada glanced from one to another, indecision in her eyes, the last of her meat pie forgotten.

Allyn realized they were both looking to him for guidance.

He made a decision. "Lauryn is on her own. It's time we leave here and continue our journey." A lump of lead settled in his gut. Taking on the role of leader felt like he was failing Lauryn. It went against his instincts to walk away and let her find her own way.

Dropping a few coins on the table, Allyn stood. The others followed him.

Days ago, when they had arrived in Losen Harbor, Jarell had scoped out the town. So, in no time they made their way to a stable that they knew hired out horses. They paid for the mounts. Then, strapping on their packs, they mounted on three sturdy mountain horses.

Allyn followed the map Allyria had given them, annotated by Father. They took the well-marked trail that ascended from the foothills into the higher mountains.

Although it was mid-spring, they donned heavy cloaks to keep away the biting wind.

Days passed. Reaching the higher altitudes, a snow squall caught them off guard.

They huddled in their cloaks below an under-hanging of rock. The horses' breath came out in puffs. The animals stood between them and the worst of the storm.

Allyn kept an arm around Giada, who shivered. Living as she did in the warm southern climate, she wasn't used to the cold.

As suddenly as it had come, the snow slowed, then stopped completely. To everyone's relief, the sun peeked out.

Allyn suggested they walk for a while, leading the horses, to get their circulation going.

When he and Jarell deemed it too steep, they mounted again and continued for a few hours. The path narrowed to a ledge with a steep drop on the left. They cautiously traversed it single file until they came to a split in the trail. One way continued forward, the other up a slanted slope.

His fingers numb, Allyn pulled out the map. No split was marked on it.

Jarell took one glance at Allyn's face and groaned. "Great, just great. Did we come the wrong way"

"Look!" Giada cried. "Isn't that another trail below us?"

Shading his eyes against the sunny, snow-blinding slope, Allyn could barely make out a winding path fifty feet below them.

"I don't know how to get down there." He could hear the frustration lacing his voice. A day wasted at the very least. "We had better go back." Allyn turned his horse around.

Giada, who had been trailing behind, now led. The ledge was narrow with a cliff on the left and a steep drop on the right. Allyn couldn't pass Jarell and Giada to get in front.

Fortunately, Giada was a good horsewoman. Her province of Samarantha bred the best horses in Valdeor. Giada had learned to ride almost as soon as she learned to walk.

After half an hour, she abruptly stopped, her mare acting skittish.

To Allyn's dismay, she dismounted and crawled to the end of the ledge, her gaze on something below.

"Giada! What are you doing?"

He couldn't hear the start of her sentence. "—The poor thing is trapped." She lay on her belly and stared into a crevice.

Jarell dismounted and held his mount still. Slipping off his own horse, Allyn squeezed past Jarell and both animals and went to join Giada. Lying beside her, he looked into the dark crevice a foot below the trail and saw two yellow eyes blinking at him. A creature had gotten wedged in the crack.

Giada grasped it around its middle and pulled it free. It looked like a large, black kitten. In the mountains? *A baby jagwaro!*

It mewled.

They glanced at it, then each other.

A spine-tingling screech echoed through the mountains.

Heart racing, Allyn and Giada flipped over to look at the rocky ledge jutting out above them. A large jagwaro crouched, its sharp teeth visible.

Jarell yelled, "Get away from there!"

The jagwaro adult yowled again.

Giada screamed. Allyn's gut clenched as he threw himself on top of her, expecting claws to rake him any second.

A deep rumbling sound followed. A huge whoosh of snow hurtled past them, chunks hitting Allyn on the back. A horse's scream grew distant.

After several moments of a thunderous roar, a heavy silence enveloped them. Buried in the cold snow, fingers of panic crawled up Allyn's spine. It was akin to drowning, only in a solid substance. Struggling, Allyn clawed the snow until his head popped above it. He drew in a gulp of air. The ledge above had blocked the worst of the avalanche.

He felt around for Giada. Finding her, he dug her out. He grasped her upper arms and pulled her up into a sitting position.

"Giada, is anything broken?"

She looked at him wordlessly, shock evident at their near death. He ran his hands over her arms and legs, feeling for breaks, but found none.

Standing up, he saw Jarell, white-faced, a few yards away. He had pressed himself and his horse against an indent in the rock wall where the ledge above jutted out the farthest. He held his horse by the reins. The mare trembled in every limb. Allyn saw no sign of his or Giada's horses.

The brothers shared looks of relief at the sight of each other.

"The big cat went over the edge with the avalanche,"

Jarell said.

Another mewling sound brought Allyn's gaze back to the squirming cub Giada still held. Tears streaked her face. "I am so sorry. This is all my fault. I should have stayed home." She gulped, letting the tears flow. "If we die here—"

"We won't!" Allyn gripped her upper arm and helped her to her feet.

Giada soothed the cub with words and stroking its back.

Meanwhile, Allyn and his brother took stock of their supplies. One waterskin, some dried food, a rope in the saddlebag and a single blanket rolled on the remaining horse. Jarell had a flint and a few odds and ends in his vest pockets, and Giada had her mini dagger and jeweled hairpins in her pocket. Allyn carried a few coins in a pouch and Uncle Guy's ring on a string around his neck. All of them had retained their weapons belted on their person, and their cloaks.

The avalanche blocked their way forward, so there was nothing for it but to turn around and head back to the split.

Forced to walk, while Giada rode the only horse, it took them much longer to reach the fork in the trail. With so much lost, Allyn wished he had never decided to try to find the missed trail.

A true leader wouldn't have made such a costly error. Lauryn would've consulted the map every step of the way.

She wouldn't have blindly relied on her judgment.

But he'd carry on, mistake or no mistake, and make the best of their circumstances.

He paused at the fork. "The upper path looks like it leads to the snowfield that swept over us. So, forward it is."

The trail sloped gradually down. The sun was well advanced when they turned a corner and the path ended. This time an old rockslide blocked their way.

Stunned, they stood defeated. Allyn's shoulders slumped.

"Look!" Jarell's enthusiasm sounded out of place. Was he suffering from altitude sickness? Why else would he sound excited?

Jarell shook Allyn's arm. "The canyon! It's in the shape of a crescent!"

Staring where Jarell pointed, Allyn studied the landscape. The canyon spread out in front of them in the shape of a crescent. Half Moon Canyon.

The path below was roughly twenty-five feet beneath where they stood. Natural fissures interspersed the canyon wall. Allyn knew that in one such fissure, Father had found the entrance to the cave at the heart of the volcanic mountain range.

The three of them shared desperate glances. They couldn't go forward and they couldn't go back.

Should they risk the third option?

Rappel down.

When he explained his idea, Jarell agreed, although Giada was unsure.

Allyn wrapped the rope around a boulder for leverage.

Jarell, nimble as a mountain goat, went first. He took the supplies slung in a satchel over his shoulder.

Pulling the rope back up, Allyn stood in front of Giada. He twitched seeing the jagwaro cub in her arms staring at him. She had managed to calm it down and it purred in her arms.

"She will die without her mama." Giada still had a haunted look in her eyes.

"It is her or us." Allyn spoke gently but firmly.

Tears gleamed in her eyes as she nodded and put the cat down. Immediately, it began exploring.

He tied the rope under her arms while giving her instructions. "I am going to lower you. Try to kick off any jutting rocks. Don't look down. Jarell is waiting for you at the base." He encouraged her to crawl over the edge.

When she seemed frozen, he projected as much confidence as he could at her. He said softly, "Trust me, Giada. You can do this."

Her eyes staring into his, as if she were drowning and he was her lifeline, she swallowed and crawled on her hands and knees backwards. The cub cried as she disappeared over the edge.

When she hung by her hands, he told her to let go of the edge and grab the rope. He played out the rope until he felt a tug letting him know she reached bottom. Leaving the rope dangling, he wrapped his hands and legs around it and prepared to rappel down.

Something hit his shoulder and claws pierced him. He saw the cub clinging to his right shoulder. It balanced there as he descended.

When he reached the other two, Giada's eyes lit up when she saw the jagwaro. She reached for it and cuddled it against her. Her smile was worth the pricks of the cat's claws.

"I'm going to name her Mystic."

Jarell stopped what he was doing and faced Giada. "You know, you can't take her home with you."

"You're not in charge of me. In fact—"

Allyn cut off her heated reply. "We don't have time for this. Let's get moving before it becomes dark."

Allyn gave a last glance up. He hated leaving the horse behind, but depending on what they found, they might have to climb back up and find another way off the mountain. Even so, their lives were more valuable than the animal's.

They made their way through the canyon, looking for an entrance into the mountain. As they approached the far end, the crescent canyon came to a dead end.

Giada leaned wearily against the rock wall. Mystic jumped from her arms and went exploring.

"Surely this is the right place!" Jarell's jaw muscle twitched, a sure sign of his frustration.

The sun had disappeared, and with it any warmth.

Allyn's limbs grew heavy with failure. "We have to find shelter," he said aloud. Or we'll freeze to death. He glanced back the way they had come.

One moment Giada stood beside him, but when he turned back to speak to her, she had disappeared.

"Allyn! Jarell!" Her voice rang out seemingly from the dead end.

Positioning himself against the wall where she had been leaning, Allyn saw her standing in a narrow opening. She moved back onto the ledge.

"We need a light," Allyn told Jarell.

His brother quickly lit the torch from his pack with his flint. He managed to squeeze through the crack.

Allyn heard breathing as Giada came behind them. They found themselves in a room-sized cave. An opening at the far end led farther into the mountain.

Giada hugged herself and grinned. "This looks like the right cave."

"A hidden entrance! Let's see where it goes!" Jarell bounced with sudden energy.

As much as he wanted to continue, Allyn, as leader, had to be the practical one. "I think we should eat and rest before exploring."

Jarell argued that they should keep on.

"Even though you are bursting with curiosity, that doesn't mean we have the energy to delve deep into the mountain. Father said he walked for hours. And we don't have unlimited torches, so we cannot rest once we enter."

Pulling out a clay jar from his satchel, Jarell grinned. "I brought something to help us. This will burn for hours. Let me light the wick hanging out of it."

"Won't the string burn out?" Giada moved closer to look at it.

"No, the oil soaking it will help keep it alight."

"We still need some rest first," Allyn insisted.

Jarell reluctantly agreed when Giada overruled him, adding her voice in favor of rest.

Allyn motioned them to sit in a row to share heat since they had no way to make a fire. They ate a portion of rations, then put out the torch. They huddled in their cloaks to get some sleep.

Allyn awoke to Jarell shaking him.

Moonlight gleaming through the cave mouth made a sinuous finger of light on the floor.

Jarell struck his flint and relit the torch.

At the sudden light, Giada rubbed sleep from her eyes. She stood and frantically searched the cave.

"What is it? Have you lost something?" Jarell sounded impatient.

"Mystic. She's gone."

"You didn't expect to keep her as a pet, did you?" Jarell rolled his eyes. "She's a wildcat, Giada. She belongs here in the mountains."

Reaching up, she wiped away a tear. "I thought since her mother was lost in the avalanche..."

Allyn thought the cat more trouble than it was worth but wouldn't say it aloud. When girls cried, it made him uncomfortable. His voice was brisk as a result. "Are we ready to find the cave?"

Jarell replied enthusiastically. Giada sniffed but nodded.

They determined to light Jarell's lamp only when the torch failed.

One by one they entered the narrow crack, Allyn leading the way, and Jarell covering their rear. The fissure had shiny, black obsidian walls. Eventually the crack opened into an enormous cave of granite. With no intersecting tunnels, Allyn had no fear of getting lost. At the far end of the cave, the path wound down and down, deeper under the mountain.

After two hours of traveling, they came to steps cut from stone as the torch began to flicker.

Jarell lit his lamp. The shadows danced eerily until the wick burnt steadily. "I'll lead."

After a long descent, the trail leveled out. Around several bends, the path widened into an enormous room of stalactites and stalagmites. All the colors of the rainbow glittered from the walls.

Giada gasped.

"Wow! Are those real jewels?" Jarell approached a cluster of twinkling red gems embedded in the wall.

Allyn bent to pick up green gems at his feet. "Amazing! This is a king's ransom. Why has this been left here after the trouble to carve those stairs?"

"And I thought the royal treasury of Samarantha was impressive." Giada sounded giddy as she picked up emeralds and amethysts.

They forgot everything else and exclaimed over each new find as they explored the cave.

"This is where the heartstones are said to originate." Jarell stuffed gems in his pockets. "Now that we're here, I can believe it."

Something bothered Allyn. He ignored it as he picked up what looked like a diamond. It must weigh a pound. *Unbelievable.*

But an insistent thought kept trying to break through his avarice. The dazzling gems kept him from remembering something. He closed his eyes to the treasure scattered around. Concentrating on taking several deep breaths, he cleared his mind.

'Avoid the allure of the vast wealth.' Allyria's voice sounded in his memory.

They weren't here for the gems.

Snapping his eyes open, Allyn crossed over to Jarell. "This isn't why we came."

Not responding, Jarell moved like one in a dream. Allyn

shook his arm. After several tries, Jarell's eyes slowly focused on him.

Glancing around, Allyn sought out Giada. She was nowhere in sight.

"Giada!" His cry echoed back to him.

A strange noise followed on his call.

"What was that?"

He motioned for Jarell to remain quiet. He listened to hear if Giada answered, but only the dripping of water cut through the heavy silence.

He hunted through the cavern, Jarell on his heels.

In his haste, Allyn nearly stumbled over her. Giada lay sleeping on the edge of a pond. *The mirror pool!*

As he bent to wake her, a slithering noise whispered at the edge of his awareness.

"We aren't alone." Jarell clutched his sword, spinning in place.

"What?" Allyn lifted his gaze and saw something move in his peripheral vision. A primal instinct made him stand and unsheathe the Crestin sword.

Placing his lamp on a broken stalagmite, Jarell swung around suddenly. "There!" He pointed.

Sucking in his breath, Allyn saw a giant salamander, as big as a man, flicking its tail before it scampered out of the light.

Allyn spun in a circle, staring at shadows beyond the lamplight. When the creature darted out from behind a formation, Allyn hacked at it. He felt his blade slice through flesh. Then the creature flashed away.

It popped out in front of Jarell, tongue flicking and claws extended. Jarell slashed at it.

While the salamander focused on his brother, Allyn attacked it from the side. Another strike.

The creature turned on Allyn, its mouth clamping on his leg. Poisonous amphibian! He hacked at it, fear coursing through his veins.

Jarell whooped a war cry and leapt on its back slashing downward. His blade must have pierced through its heart because the creature spasmed a few times and flopped dead.

The jaws of the salamander loosened, and Allyn pushed it off of him.

Jarell squatted next to him and pulled a pouch of dried leaves from a vest pocket. "Here. Chew on them since I can't boil them. But they should counteract any deadly toxins."

The herbs tasted bitter but Allyn choked them down with a swig of water.

"What else do you have in your vest?"

Jarell grinned back at him. "Things you'd never think to bring."

Giada sat up, yawning. Her glance fell on their bloody blades. Her eyes widened, all sleepiness fleeing. "What happened to you?"

"If you hadn't chose a strange time to take a nap, you would have seen the giant salamander that attacked us."

Jarell's voice had an edge to it.

Giada glanced around and blanched at the sight of the dead monster yards from her. She scurried to Allyn's side. "The sooner we get out of here, the better!"

"But we haven't learned what we came for." Allyn motioned to the pond. "We need the location of the firebird."

A gleam in her eye, Giada gave a tantalizing smile. "You haven't been the only busy ones. I must've fallen into an enchanted sleep. I dreamt its location. Now, let's get out of here before I have hysterics. I hate lizards."

"Salamander," Jarell corrected her.

"Whatever! Creepy thing." She shuddered.

Picking up the lamp with one hand and carrying his sword in the other, Jarell led the way. This time they ignored the twinkling jewels. Could there be more giant salamanders in the cavern waiting for a meal?

But finding the exit wasn't simple. They had wandered all over the cavern. Multiple tunnels lead away from it. Which was the right one?

They spent half an hour following one tunnel only to end up back in the cave of gems.

Allyn limped along after Jarell. This is why he would make a terrible leader. He should've marked the tunnel when they first arrived. Lauryn wouldn't have made the same error.

"This place is suffocating." Giada clung to Allyn's arm.

After she pointed it out, Allyn did feel the weight of the

mountain pressing upon him, causing him to sweat. If not for the little light, he might share her fear. This chamber could be their grave.

6 Ransom

It seemed as if she had been a prisoner forever, but Lauryn acknowledged it had probably been forty-five minutes that she sat in the bottom of the boat while her captors rowed away from her friends. The oars slapped rhythmically. Around a headland, a ship came into view, anchored in a bay. The smaller boat headed for it.

As they pulled alongside it, the crew lowered down a rope ladder. Lauryn's captor flung her like a sack of potatoes over his shoulder and climbed up into the ship. She squeezed her eyes shut at the upside-down view.

With her hands tied in front of her, she felt for her dagger on her belt when he set her down. Gone! He must've taken it.

The unkempt look of the sailors had her heart thundering. Pirates!

Her captor gripped her arm and yanked her through the crowd of sailors gathered. "Make way. Captain Yeager needs to see our prize."

The gathered men moved aside, leering at her. She expected them to make raucous comments, but they only eyed her silently.

Her captor stopped in front of a short, swarthy man who Lauryn took to be the leader. Dark curls poked out of his sweat-stained kerchief. He wore a cutlass at his waist. Lauryn's gut roiled at the pirate's brawny form, with his corded, bare arms which could easily crush her.

His cruel eyes raked her from head to toe. He circled around her.

"You should bring a hefty ransom. What think you, men?"

They cheered and whistled.

Captain Yeager grinned at her fear, and she noticed the beads in his braided beard. "How much will your parents pay for your return, princess?"

The pirates called out ridiculous amounts with bawdy jokes.

Lauryn swallowed. How did he know her identity? She clenched her hands to keep them from trembling.

The captain chuckled.

He held out a hand and the pirates quieted.

He came close to her and leaned over, pretending to whisper in her ear. "Don't worry, doll. We won't hurt you. You're worth more untouched." Captain Yeager guffawed and his men joined in, but she didn't like the hungry look in their eyes.

"Take her below." He motioned to her captor.

"Yes, Cap'n Yeager!"

Without glancing to see if his man obeyed, Yeager strode off, calling orders to set sail.

The pirate led her down into the hold, stopping at a door. He untied her hands, and roughly pushed her in, slamming the door and locking it.

Lauryn leaned against it. *This couldn't be the end of the quest for her. It just couldn't. She wouldn't just wait to be shipped back home after her parents paid the ransom.*

With nothing to do all day, trapped in the cabin where they put her, Lauryn turned her mind over who could have betrayed her.

Not Irdek. Mother had saved him from dying when he was a child. He had spoken of Mother with nothing but gratitude. Same for his mother Irda. She had convinced Marjek to let Mother concoct an herbal remedy for Irdek when Mother and Father had been shipwrecked on the island. And the blind Nyrmidion tribal leader, Marjek Red Horns, himself had kept faith with Valdeor since those days.

Not Everard. A close family friend, he was more like an older brother to her than a royal guard. Besides, Father had sent him along to protect her. Though, she only had Everard's word for that. Father hadn't mentioned anything to her before they left.

Lauryn shook herself. Shame gripped her. Everard, her Everard, would never harm her.

That left Xylander.

What did she know of Xylander? Very little. Their countries had been enemies for centuries.

Mother had crossed paths with the future ruler of Canteor, Princess Sefira, when Uncle Guy found the mysterious Isle of Origin. Only weeks after Lauryn's birth, Mother and Xylander's grandfather, King Pashmi, at Princess Sefira's urging, had signed an accord. Quite a miraculous feat at that time.

So, Xylander had no motive.

Her thoughts strayed. Why was he even tagging along?

A thought niggled at the back of Lauryn's mind. She was missing something.

Aunt Donella had a certain look in her eyes when she insisted Xylander come along. The look she got when...match-making.

Lauryn leapt to her feet. Match-making! Like pieces of a puzzle, it fell into place. Aunt Donella wanted to give her and Xylander a chance to know each other.

She paced in the small space, unable to calm herself.

Her ire rose as she rejected the idea of Xylander as a possible consort. Arrogant, overconfident, derisive.

But she had been trained to put her realm over her own desires. And as much as she didn't like him on a personal level, she couldn't help categorizing the advantages such an alliance would bring. It would strengthen the ties between the two countries.

Canteor still had places where pagans worshiped the god Panmin, nearly twenty years after witnessing the miracles the One Who Fashioned All had performed. An influx of priests, bringing religious customs from Valdeor, would help the citizens turn from their false god.

Souls were at stake.

Her heart stuttered. Lauryn put her head in her hands. She desperately wanted to pray to the One Who Fashioned All not to make this her future. She had no feelings for Xylander.

She grasped for straws. He was younger than she. She did the calculations in her head. Well, if she was honest, he was only ten months younger.

She wrestled with herself. She'd prefer her brother's best friend, her long-time crush, over the foreigner. But what if Xylander was the better choice for Valdeor's citizens?

"Thy will be done," she forced herself to pray.

Peace settled over her. If she examined the issue, she had plenty of time before her parents called on her to make a marriage alliance. She was only seventeen!

And Xylander seemed to prefer Giada. Not only that. As future rulers of their respective countries, on continents separated by hundreds of miles of seas, it wouldn't work.

Now, if Allyn won and she lost...

She refused to go there. *Another reason to win this contest!*

She paced again. Her mind went back to the problem at

hand. If no one she considered had conspired with the pirates, it meant someone close to Irdek had betrayed him. One of his own tribe. That made more sense.

For two days, Lauryn sat or paced, trying to come up with a plan to escape. The only interaction she had was the daily meal delivery.

On the third day, Lauryn heard a key in the lock. She glanced around the tiny cabin again. She longed for a weapon, but the room had been stripped of anything useful.

Two men appeared in the doorway. One of them eyed her, not saying a word. He put some bread and a pitcher on the floor. The other blocked the only way out. Then they closed and locked the door behind him before she could ask him anything.

Her chances of escaping the pirate ship? Non-existent. She would wait until they transferred her to land.

She ate the bread and greedily drank the stale water. It quenched her thirst. Not long after, her head began to swim. She fought to keep her eyes open. *Had they drugged the water?*

Stupid not to anticipate that.

Lauryn awoke to darkness. Something felt strange. The floor no longer heaved. Her eyes adjusted to the dimness. She could see a covered window, light leaking around the edges.

Her hands weren't tied together, but her right wrist

wore a...*bracelet?*

Scratchy straw underneath her made her itch. The floor was made of stone, not planks. They must've transferred her to a building while she slept.

Close at hand, a pitcher sat. Her throat burned, but she wouldn't drink the water, even though it smelled fresh. She did dip her hands in it and splash her face, avoiding her eyes, in case it was drugged.

Lauryn wobbled as she stood. She tried to focus, but fog filled her mind. She walked about six feet before her bracelet prevented her from advancing. Not a bracelet. A manacle! Following the links back in the dark, she discovered she had been chained to a bolt in the stone wall. She walked the chain's length from one corner of the room to the other. She only got halfway to the door and the window. She yanked, but the chain held steady.

The little stone room had no furniture. Only straw for her to lie on.

Hearing footsteps, she crouched down, ready to spring.

She heard the scrape of a lock opening, then she saw two burly men outlined in the doorway. One stood guard outside, while the other entered.

She drew back from the greasy-haired man wearing tattered breeches as he came close.

Looking at the full pitcher, he chided. "Ye need to keep up yer strength, girly." He put down a couple of pieces of fruit and unwrapped a chunk of bread from a kerchief he pulled from his pocket.

Lauryn measured from his exposed dagger to the man outside. Her shoulders sagged. No way to overpower two men, not without a proper weapon. If it had been one man, she would have used the chain to choke him when he turned to leave, grabbed his dagger, and the keys. She would have to wait for a better chance.

Once they departed, she bit into the fruit. Juice ran down her chin. She hoped the liquid would stave off her thirst, because she was loath to drink the water.

Hours later, the sweltering afternoon humidity and thickness of her tongue tempted her to sip a little. Even stale and warm, she couldn't resist drinking more than she thought good for her.

She paced in a half circle at the chain's limit. No one knew her location. No one was going to save her. She'd have to save herself. Her best chance of escape was at night.

Time dragged while she waited for darkness.

Lauryn reached up to her large hair barrette, which, surprisingly, the pirates hadn't touched. Satisfaction rushed through her when her fingers pulled out the tiny dirk hidden within it.

She picked at the manacle's lock. After a number of tries, she released herself.

Trying the door, she found it locked. No surprise. Next, she went to the window. It was shuttered from the outside, but she managed to rattle it. Using the small blade, she positioned it in the crack between the shutters. She jiggled it until the outer latch loosened.

She slowly pushed one side far enough that she could spy the area. The window opened toward the sea. She could see the waves gently crashing in the moonlight. The fresh breeze lifted tendrils of her damp hair.

The window stood roughly fifteen feet above the ground. The area below was lightly covered with vegetation.

She set herself to watch for a sentry. Ten, fifteen, twenty minutes slowly passed. She waited for an hour by her reckoning. The guard passed by twice in that time.

After his second pass, she was ready. Ever so carefully, she pushed the shutter open until she could wiggle through. Sitting on the edge, she lowered herself over until she hung by her fingertips. Less than ten feet to the ground below.

Dropping soundlessly, she landed on a bush that broke her fall. She'd feel the scratches later, but energy coursed through her, numbing her to the sting. She edged around the building. She peeked around the corner to see if a sentry had been posted. Sure enough, a big lout sat outside the main door, snoring.

The building sat at the wilderness's edge. A few dwellings huddled together nearby. In the bay beyond them, the pirate's vessel lay anchored. Lights and sound came from it, even though the positions of the stars let her know that the night was advanced.

A smaller ship's sails glinted outside the harbor, drifting

toward the shore. Friendlies or reinforcements?

Lauryn glanced at the jungle. She'd take her chances and run for it.

But first she cautiously approached the sentry, smelling strongly of ale. Though she longed for his cutlass, he would surely awaken if she tried to remove it. Pulse throbbing, she carefully pulled his dagger from his waistband. He snorted and changed position. Her heart leapt into her throat and she froze.

Glancing around, she made sure nobody had come into view.

The only movement was the second ship as it drew into the harbor.

By now, the guard had settled back to sleep.

She finished slipping the dagger away from him and ran inland.

Finding a trail of sorts, she plunged into the jungle, the dagger held ready for new threats.

Half an hour later, she heard pursuit behind her. They must've discovered her absence! No use trying for stealth anymore. She took off running, crashing through the brush. Panic welled as the running feet came nearer.

"Lauryn! Are you there?"

Tears welled in her eyes at the familiar voice. She came to a halt, a stitch in her side. "I'm here!"

In a few moments, Everard came into view, Xylander trailing behind. Everard caught her up in a bear hug. For a moment, a warm feeling of safety enveloped her as he held her tight.

Xylander watched them with a scowl. He kept one eye on the path behind him.

"Ever! Am I glad to see you!" She couldn't help gushing, as if she were Allyria's age.

"I know... You can't live without me." Everard released her with a smirk. But his eyes gleamed with relief as he looked her over.

Embarrassment made her momentarily mute.

"How did you find me?" "What happened to you?" they said simultaneously.

"When we couldn't find you, I saw a small boat rowing out to sea." Everard frowned at the memory. "We figured you must be on board. Irdek brought us here on his ship."

She thought she'd seen a figure on the cliff when the pirates abducted her from Irdek's village.

"We saw someone escape as we came ashore. Xylander and I agreed it could only be you. This was the only path you could've taken." He looked her over. "Are you all right? Did those beasts hurt you?"

Lauryn wanted to be held and comforted more but she forced herself to take command. "I'm fine. I'll tell you what happened later. First, let's get back to your ship."

Everard coaxed her forward, not back. "Xylander and I

swam ashore."

Only then did she realize the dampness she felt came from his embrace, not the humid air.

"Our shipmates are circling the island," he continued. "They told us a place where the *Valiant* can land and we can meet up."

"I can't believe you escaped on your own." Xylander seemed amazed that she hadn't waited for them to show up.

She held back an unladylike snort with an effort.

"Do you have any water?" Lauryn's thirst made her head throb. Xylander handed her his waterskin and she drank deeply.

As they walked farther away from the pirate's lair, Lauryn told them everything that happened since they parted.

"As soon as I realized you weren't with us, I searched for you." Everard's voice thickened with concern. "They didn't hurt you, did they?" He gently touched her arm, fear for her etched on his face, as his eyes searched hers for the truth.

"No. They just drugged me."

Some of the tenseness in his posture bled away. "Fought like a wildcat, did you?" Everard grinned and draped his arm over her shoulders.

She hadn't thought it prudent to do so, but let him think it. She basked in his approval.

Xylander, in the lead, glanced back at her. Lauryn couldn't tell if he was pleased or horrified.

"When we couldn't find you," Everard continued, "Irdek recognized one of the rival warriors. He guessed the attack on his town was a ploy to abduct you."

They came to a fork in the trail. Everard used the stars to determine which direction to head to the meeting cove. They soon overlooked a bay that had a large stone stack off the point. He insisted they rest. Irdek's ship, the *Valiant*, would be there well before dawn.

Everard took the first watch. Huddled against a tree trunk, Lauryn didn't think she'd sleep but she did. Ever was here and she no longer carried the burden alone. She was able to relax enough to drift off.

In the hour before the sun rose, Xylander woke them. They picked their way down to the cove. They hadn't gone far when they heard a snuffling noise, a squeal following. Hooves pounded their way.

The hair along Lauryn's arms rose.

A large boar burst from the brush thirty feet away. Five feet long with sharp tusks, the beast's little pig eyes glared at them.

"Climb!" Everard pushed her toward a tree.

Needing no encouragement, Lauryn scrambled up from branch to branch. She looked for a loose branch she could use as a weapon. A fragrance tickled her nose as she huddled on a limb, a cluster of nuts hanging nearby. She gathered handfuls of them to use as missiles.

Everard had climbed another tree, not as large as hers.

It bent with his weight.

Sucking in her breath, Lauryn realized Xylander stood on the path with his drawn sword. "Xylander! Get to safety!"

Too late! The boar, seeing him, charged.

Xylander, with surprising grace, somersaulted over the boar, slashing its back legs upon landing. Squealing and spinning around, the angered swine pawed the ground, grunted and charged although he dragged one hamstrung leg.

As it came near to goring Xylander, the prince jumped aside, his blade scoring the boar's side.

Everard dropped from his tree behind the beast. He pierced it with his sword.

The beast turned to rend Everard.

Taking aim, Lauryn pelted the boar with a dozen nutmegs, one after another, to distract it. Meanwhile, Xylander came from the side and speared the boar through the heart. It collapsed.

Swinging down from the tree, Lauryn joined the boys. She prickled all over at its size up close.

"That was the bravest, yet most foolhardy thing I've ever seen. You showed amazing acrobatics and swordsmanship!" She had misjudged the arrogant prince, thinking his skill with a scimitar was boastfulness. But she was willing to admit her mistake to him.

"But next time, please climb a tree." Everard wiped his brow.

Xylander cracked an unexpected smile. "What, so you can impress Lauryn with your skill?"

Without skipping a beat, Everard smirked. "She is already aware of my superior swordsmanship. That is why I came along."

Lauryn rolled her eyes. Although they both secretly impressed her, she'd never let on. No need to further puff up their male pride.

Once, just once, Lauryn would like to see Everard discomposed.

As dawn broke, Lauryn, Everard, and Xylander came out near the headland jutting out into the deep blue ocean. On the horizon, smudges indicated more islands in the chain.

No one was about.

They crouched at the jungle's edge, watching distant sails approach.

"Shall we persuade the captain to head for Hamleor and find Allyn?" Lauryn glanced between Xylander and Everard. "He is sure to have found the Half Moon canyon and mirror pool by now." Which meant he had a head start over her. Knowing she could lose to Allyn galled her.

Xylander cleared his throat. They both gave him their attention. Xylander almost looked apologetic as he rubbed his hand through his hair. "There is no need to gaze into the mountain pond. I know where a firebird resides."

Stunned, Lauryn closed her mouth when she realized it hung open. "You do? Then why didn't you say so days ago?" *Really! What deceitfulness, holding out on them!*

"I didn't know if I could trust you." He glanced from one to the other. His face softened. "It is a well-guarded secret in my land. The firebird is a symbol of undying strength. We don't speak of it to outsiders."

She didn't like it, but she understood his reason. As eldest, she held secrets of national safety. Things she couldn't even tell her younger siblings, or Everard.

"Your secret is safe with us. We won't break your trust." Lauryn projected her princess of the realm persona as she spoke for both herself and Everard.

"Then set sail for Canteor. I will be your guide."

"Is that why Aunt Donella invited you to join our expedition? Not to..." she trailed off. She had thought the Waykeeper meant to throw them together. Her cheeks burned thinking of it.

Everard gave her a strange look.

She glanced away from their stares.

Gazing at the horizon, Lauryn couldn't focus. Spots danced before her eyes. She rubbed them. Her limbs grew heavy. She suddenly clutched her head.

"Lauryn? Are you ill?" Everard's voice sounded concerned. He put his hand on her forehead. She had trouble focusing on his face.

"Does she still suffer from the drugs the pirates gave

her?" Even Xylander sounded worried. Or perhaps he feared she would lose her stomach's contents.

"It's too long for her to still feel the drug's effects. Did you eat or drink anything recently, Lauryn?" Everard ordered her to drink water from his waterskin.

"I don't feel nauseous, but strangely lethargic."

Sipping water, Lauryn could only come up with one explanation for the sudden onset of dizziness. "I think I am feeling what Allyn is feeling."

Xylander scowled at her. "She's delirious."

"No. You don't understand. Allyn is my twin. We have a connection. When I broke my leg, Allyn knew it and came looking for me. When his horse threw him in a hunt, I had a feeling something bad happened." She glanced from Everard to Xylander. "I can't explain it any better."

"I've occasionally seen it working between the two of you." Everard tried to urge her to lie down, but she refused.

Slowly the cloudiness passed from her mind. She could only pray that all was well with Allyn.

"Look!" Xylander jumped up from his crouching position, pointing toward the sea. "Retreat!" He moved further into the jungle.

Lauryn heard Everard gasp. Then he pulled her up and half-dragged her into the bushes.

She glanced out to sea. A ship! But it wasn't the small vessel she had seen last night that had deposited her companions. The pirate ship that captured her moved to block the bay mouth. Men lowered the dinghy and pirates sailed into the cove.

"Quickly, head back inland!" Everard kept a hold of her arm and towed her along with him.

As they approached the trail, men spilled from the dinghy, spreading out along the beach. Soon, they blocked the way back. The dense jungle thwarted their efforts to run. The pirates searched the brush.

Nowhere to hide! Too many enemies against two swords.

Surrounded by pirates, Lauryn's hope deserted her, like sand washed out to sea.

7 Sail to Canteor

*T*wo more tunnels dead-ended.

Back in the main cavern, Jarell scratched a mark on the tunnel wall when they exited it. "At least we won't try this one again."

The glinting gems and weird shadows cast by the lamp threw a gloom over Allyn's soul. He couldn't believe he had thought their cold beauty alluring.

Allyn's leg throbbed. He felt sluggish. The salamander venom must be working through his system. Jarell's lamp was more than half spent, and they still had hours before they could make it to the surface, even if they found the right tunnel to the surface. Allyn wouldn't share his worry with the two younger ones.

If only he had noted a landmark as they entered. He searched his memory for anything they encountered when they found the cave of gems.

Wait. Two stalagmites side by side.

Scanning the room, Allyn saw three tunnels with two stalagmites near them. He pointed to the nearest pair. "Let's try this way."

"We're lost, aren't we?" Giada's voice trembled.

"We'll be fine. We have food and there's water down here." Allyn projected a cheerful attitude that he didn't feel.

Jarell met his eyes over the lamp. The look he gave Allyn meant he was aware the words were meant to soothe Giada, not a true assessment of their predicament. His brother wasn't the most tactful person, so Allyn was relieved when Jarell didn't blurt the truth. *A small amount of food left. And once the light failed, all hope of leaving died.*

They entered the fissure by the two stalagmites. Allyn was sure this tunnel was the right one until it started descending. It should go up.

An odd smell assaulted him. He tried to place it. Noxious. Reptilian. Allyn sensed danger in the suffocating blackness. He thought he heard a rustle in the distance.

"We need to head back." He tried to keep his voice calm.

Grumbling, Jarell turned around. Another sound and they all froze.

"Out! Quick!" Allyn whispered urgently.

They ran back the way they had come. The cave of gems was cool in comparison. But the incessant drip rubbed Allyn's nerves raw.

Perspiration dripped down his back.

More time lost. The lamp in Jarell's hand burnt lower.

A soft mewling sound echoed around the chamber. Allyn drew his sword and faced the fissure they had exited. Another salamander!

Giada took off in the other direction.

"Giada! Where are you going?" Allyn's gut clenched at her danger. "It's not safe!"

"Don't you hear her? Mystic is showing us the way out!"

A louder mewling echoed in the cavern. Giada cried joyfully. "Sweetie! You found us. Good girl!"

And so they followed the jagwaro up through the stair cut into the mountain. And when Jarell's lamp flickered near the end of its oil, Allyn put one hand on the wall and held Giada's hand with the other. Jarell grabbed her other hand. Fortunately, they were past the stairs and the floor was smooth. Soon they walked in the endless dark. Since there had been no other tunnels breaking off this one, Allyn knew they couldn't get lost.

The darkness pressed mightily on them, and the edge of panic brushed him.

Wooziness made him stumble. *So hot. Need air. Light. Must get out!*

"Sing for us, Giada. You have a beautiful voice."

"I-I can't. This place is too awful." He could hear the fear in her trembling voice.

Surprisingly, Jarell started singing a jaunty tune more suited to Christmastime. But soon they all joined in, warbling at first then growing more confident. They sang all the verses they could remember of popular songs. Their repertoire depleted, Allyn realized he saw a dim light ahead.

After fifteen minutes of forcing one foot in front of the

other, Allyn's fingers ran out of wall.

Giada knocked into Allyn's back as he came to a stop.

Allyn took a few steps forward and blinked in the narrow strip of light. After hours of total darkness, the dim cave light caused him to squint.

Jarell whooped. Giada cried with relief. The jagwaro cub stalked to the exit.

Allyn fought a wave of dizziness.

Startled, he heard voices outside. He raised a hand to quiet his companions. He shuffled over to the opening, favoring his injured leg.

"I don't see any cave entrance, but the owner of the horse had to go somewhere. The beast cannot have been here long. A jagwaro or wolf would have gotten to it otherwise."

"We must have missed the entrance. Spread out and look again." Feet shuffled away.

Allyn pressed against the narrow fissure wall and peered out. Several men in thick sheep-hide jerkins were spread out along the canyon.

"Help!"

Everyone turned his way as Allyn stepped from the cave. He was near to exhaustion but he had to take care of the others.

"Companions and I...lost...in mountain." He collapsed to his knees, black dots dancing before his eyes.

Soon the mountain men surrounded them, offering food and blankets, and even a skin of wine. Somehow, they had coaxed the rented horse down into the canyon.

Allyn sweat with a fever despite the cold air. He heard Jarell tell them how they fought a giant salamander that had bitten Allyn. Fortunately, their rescuers had an antidote they administered which they promised would clear his system.

It took a day and a half, but the men escorted them to their mountain fastness, a tiny village nestled in a remote valley. Allyn was in and out of consciousness during the trip. It seemed the poison wasn't fast-acting and had been caught in time.

Allyn rested ten days, asleep for the first two. He fretted over the time lost until he recovered enough to press on.

When he insisted that he was well enough to travel, an older guide led them on borrowed horses to the trailhead leading to Losen Harbor. It took two days.

They thanked the guide, who then departed.

Another day of walking for Jarell and Giada while Allyn rode on their pack horse. Chivalrously, he wanted to let Giada ride, but she refused. In his weakened state, he knew he needed it more than she did. The next day, they got a lift the rest of the way in a wagon of hay. The farmer let them tie the horse to the back of the wagon.

Allyn turned to Giada. With her cap discarded, her blonde hair was a halo of curls around her engaging face.

"So, where do we go to find the firebird?" He kept his voice down, although the farmer was on the seat of the wagon and they were in the back.

Jarell smacked his forehead. "I can't believe I forgot about the dream you had, Giada."

She smirked at Jarell. The jagwaro in her lap yawned and curled up. "I dreamt of a beautiful purple bird sitting on its nest on a mountaintop in Canteor."

Once back in Losen Harbor, they sought to buy passage aboard the *Seaspray,* a ship sailing to Canteor. Allyn was disturbed to find he hadn't enough coins to pay for all three fares. Not after paying for the loss of two rented horses in the avalanche.

Giada offered her jeweled hairpin to him in payment. As much as he hated taking her pretty bauble, Allyn was forced to barter it. He promised himself that he would replace it for her when this was over.

Although Allyn had studied the language, history, and culture of Valdeor's former enemy, he had never been to the Canteor continent.

He wondered if Lauryn was already there ahead of him.

The antidote and the fresh sea air cleansed his system of the last of the salamander venom. The bite left a scar, a tale of his bravery.

Five days passed swiftly. Allyn used the time in sparring practice with Jarell and getting back to optimum performance. He found that prolonged use of his leg caused him to limp slightly.

He continued teaching Giada defensive tactics. She wasn't at Lauryn's skill level, or even Allyria's, but she had improved. He was surprised and relieved to learn that Jarell had kept up her training while Allyn was laid up.

In her free hours, Giada worked on teaching Mystic tricks. She insisted on keeping the jagwaro. Since it saved their lives, Allyn didn't have the heart to put his foot down and forbid her to bring it with them. The sailors were happy to have the ship's rat population under control.

Jarell liked working with the crew and learning navigation. If Allyn became the next high king, he would encourage Jarell to pursue it. Eventually, Jarell could command the royal navy.

Hearing a delighted laugh, Allyn came back to the present. He swung around until he saw Giada and Jarell at the rail, pointing with excitement at something in the water. Joining them, he saw a pod of dolphins leaping alongside the *Seaspray*. The sleek animals made high-pitched squeals of delight as they frolicked.

When they finally swam away, the dark horizon drew Allyn's attention. Lightning flashed at the heart of a large storm ahead. Although they sailed in sunshine, the waves soon became choppy.

The sailors went about their jobs with worried glances at the horizon.

"I suggest you go below, Your Highnesses." The captain's expression was grim. "This time of year we can encounter massive storms. There is no way to avoid this one, and no turning back."

Allyn shepherded an anxious Giada and serious Jarell below decks.

"Please don't leave me alone. Sit with me in my cabin." Giada pleaded.

So instead of heading to the hammocks strung in a large berthing area, the brothers joined Giada in her cabin. The attached desk and bolted chair were features in the captain's quarters. The cabin also contained a bed as well as a hammock slung in the corner.

Jarell took the hammock, while a pale-faced Giada sat cross-legged on the bed. Allyn claimed the chair bolted to the floor, sitting astride so he could converse with his brother and Giada. Soon afterward, they could hear the wind and waves, and feel their effects.

Trying to distract both Giada and themselves, the brothers told her everything they could remember from Allyria's book about the firebird and its habits. Giada, in turn, described her dream in detail. They threw out ideas on how to snatch a feather from the bird.

Hours passed in stifling heat and rollicking swells. The hour grew late and Allyn said they should retire and let her sleep.

"I cannot imagine sleeping in this storm!" Giada sent him a scared look. He couldn't resist her beautiful green eyes. So, they all ate a little hard tack in companionable silence, each with their own thoughts. They even drowsed sitting up.

Then the storm increased in fury, tossing the ship like a toy boat in a flood. Gale-force winds threatened to tear the *Seaspray* apart.

An awful-sounding crack and resounding boom brought Allyn to high alert. The *Seaspray* listed steeply to port.

Water cascaded under the door.

"Abandon ship!" a voice yelled outside their cabin.

Allyn leapt up and yanked the door open. A flood of cold water hit him. Grabbing Giada's arm as she scrambled over to him, he plowed into the narrow hall.

They followed the sailor up the steps.

Jarell appeared on Giada's other side. Holding onto the banister with one hand Allyn pulled her up through the water which was trying to push them back into the hold.

Reaching the deck they stared in dismay. The mast had broken and drifted in the sea. Giant waves washed over the deck, while heavy rain came down in sheets.

Sailors were jumping over the side.

Grasping Giada's hand with an iron grip, Allyn headed over to the edge. A swell caught his legs and pushed him overboard.

Cold water engulfed him. The shock gave him the energy to fight to the surface. Allyn kicked his legs and thrust his head out of the water. Giada bobbed beside him, gasping. He grabbed her in a swimmer's hold to keep her head above water. The dark seas tossed them this way and that.

The mast was the largest floating object but rigging lines were a hazard waiting to snare the unwary. Caught in them, one would get pulled under with the ship when it sank.

Scanning the area, he saw Jarell. His brother shouted something but he couldn't hear in the chaos. Jarell swam toward a dinghy carrying several crewmen, drifting in the waves. He climbed aboard. Allyn struck out to join him, towing Giada. When they arrived, he boosted her partway on. Several sailors reached for her and hauled her in. Allyn hefted himself onto the boat.

It was only then that he took stock of perhaps a dozen sailors already onboard. Behind them, the *Seaspray* slipped under the waves.

Time slowed to a crawl. Every moment was a fight for the dinghy to stay afloat as it rode the swells. Allyn hooked an arm around Giada as they crouched between the slatted seats.

Hours passed. It felt like a century.

Allyn somehow drifted off to sleep. Suddenly, a giant swell overturned the half-swamped dinghy. He found himself underwater. In the churn, it was hard to tell which way was up. He struggled to detect any light. He pushed his body in the way he thought he should go, the need for air his only thought. Panic subsided as he broke the surface.

It took him several moments to find the dinghy, still adrift, but upside-down. A few men clung on desperately. He struck out for it.

Reaching it, he hauled himself up. Neither his brother nor Giada were there. Using the vantage point, he wiped his eyes and searched the trough for any sign of them, praying under his breath.

There! Two heads bobbing close together. He took a deep breath and let himself slip into the water. He swam toward them. He could see Jarell flagging, as he tried keeping Giada afloat. As Allyn came beside them, Jarell let Giada go. Allyn caught her in a swimmer's hold again.

A quarter hour later, they were clinging to the flipped vessel. With another man's help, Allyn boosted Giada up so she was partly out of the water. He held onto the capsized boat, one arm securing her.

Fortunately, the rain lessened soon after, then finally stopped. The waves grew smaller. Eventually, the clouds broke and the sun shone down.

Allyn raised his head from the stupor that enveloped him.

His throat burned.

He counted nine sailors left of the crew still clinging to the capsized boat. Pieces of flotsam drifted nearby. He spotted a large cargo hatch. He reached over Giada to tap Jarell and get his attention. He pointed at the hatch. It only had room for the three of them.

"Giada," he whispered, "do you have the strength to swim?"

She squinted her salt-encrusted eyelashes at him and nodded.

He let go and waited for her to do the same. She swam alongside him to the hatch in the calm water. Jarell climbed aboard and pulled Giada up onto the makeshift raft. Allyn joined them.

Meanwhile, the remaining crewmen were trying to turn the dinghy upright.

"Look! Mystic!" Giada pointed to the bedraggled jagwaro floating on a passing crate. As it came nearer, Allyn grabbed a piece of flotsam and snagged the crate. When it was close, the wildcat leapt onto the hatch.

Allyn pulled the crate aboard and levered it open with his dagger. He looked inside to find it full of melons. Taking out three, he offered the sailors the rest. He pushed the crate overboard toward them. One sailor swam to the crate and pulled it to the waiting crewmen. They had given up trying to right the heavy, wooden dinghy, and straddled it instead.

Using his dagger, Allyn split open the fruit. He, Jarell, and Giada ravenously ate the melons, the juice helping sate their thirst.

The small miracle lifted their mood.

Afterward, they all laid down and gave their aching muscles a rest. Holding onto the upturned dinghy for hours in the storm had depleted their strength. The gentle motion of the raft lulled Allyn to sleep.

A startled cry awakened Allyn. Sitting up, his gaze landed on Jarell and Giada still asleep. His relief was momentary. Where was the danger? His gaze roamed the seas, looking for the cry's source. Allyn saw no sign of the dinghy or other survivors.

Movement snagged his gaze.

Fins cut through the water.

The wildcat made a loud screech, its fur standing on end as it watched the circling beasts of the deep.

Allyn bowed his head and prayed to the One Who Fashioned All to save them. Then he broke wood slats from the crate's lid to use as a weapon and paddle. Waking up Jarell, he urged him to help paddle toward land. They whacked the monsters when they circled nearby.

Giada sat up, her skin red with sunburn. Allyn guessed they all looked equally burnt. She huddled fearfully in the middle of the makeshift raft.

After a heart-stopping half an hour, a breeze freshened the humid air. As the water grew choppy, the fins disappeared.

As they reached the shore, Allyn and Jarell jumped off and dragged the hatch cover well up the beach in case they needed it again.

They walked along the beach until they found a fresh water rivulet emptying into the sea. They drank deeply until

119

they had eased their thirst. Allyn splashed the cool water on his face. Jarell dunked his whole head under then shook it like a hound. Giada rinsed her kerchief and wrung it out. She used it to dab her face and neck.

When they finished, Jarell pulled something small from his inner vest pocket. He studied it in his hand.

"What do you have there?" Allyn leaned over to see a small sliver of rock. Jarell filled a cupped leaf with water. The rock floated in it and spun around on its own.

"It's a lodestone. It always points true north."

Allyn looked at the sun and moon's positions and back down at the lodestone. He frowned. "But that means—"

Jarell caught his glance. "Yes. We're in the Nyrmidion Isles. The storm pushed us off course."

Allyn's gut churned. They had floated east instead of south.

Having no other recourse, Allyn decided they should walk along the shore looking for habitation.

After a few hours on the rocky beach, a promontory blocked their access. Scrambling up the sharp, basalt rocks, they made it to the other side. A large vessel floated in the harbor. Crewmen worked on the shore. Some loaded barrels, likely containing fresh water, aboard a dinghy. Others carried clusters of fruit.

"The flag is Nyrmidion." Jarell whispered excitedly.

Allyn weighed whether or not to approach the crew. "Let's see if we can get passage away from here. But we'll keep our identities secret."

The sailors spotted them when they left the cliff's safety. Several men met them as they descended to the beach. Allyn described their shipwreck, letting them know there was another boatload of survivors out there. Sympathetic, the sailors took them to their leader.

The tall, broad-shouldered man was ordering the loading of the goods onto the wooden dinghy.

The man's profile seemed familiar to Allyn. He turned to look at them.

Surprise flooded Allyn as recognition dawned.

"Irdek!" A weight lifted from Allyn's shoulders. "What good fortune for us!" He turned to Giada. "He's a friend."

Giada searched Allyn's eyes. So he squeezed her hand, letting her know she was safe.

After heartily greeting them, Irdek invited them aboard his vessel.

Soon, they were on the dinghy headed to the ship.

As the sailors maneuvered to the prow, Giada glanced at the ladder. "I can't climb up. My arms are too tired from clutching the dinghy all night."

Allyn knew he didn't have the strength to carry her. His bad leg ached. The hours spent clinging to the boat and Giada during the endless storm, had worn out his reserves.

Irdek manned the oars, his muscles bulging. "It's all right." He stood up when they bumped into the vessel. "I've got her."

Giada glanced anxiously at Allyn.

He smiled and nodded at her. "You can trust him."

Relief washed across Giada's face. She passed Mystic to Allyn and stood. She let Allyn's friend pick her up and carry her. Irdek climbed, nimble as a monkey, as if Giada weighed nothing.

Allyn, below them on the rope ladder, saw her squint her eyes shut. Her cat clung to his shoulder, and its claws dug into his leather jerkin.

Once settled on board, Irdek ordered food and dry clothes for them. They ate bread and cheese and drank hot tea.

Giada still had a haunted look about her from all they had gone through. So, Allyn sat close to her and, after he finished eating, draped an arm over her shoulders and tried to get her to relax.

"What brought you here, Irdek?" Allyn marveled that his family's friend should be the one who found them.

"The tempest pushed our ship off course. We rode out the worst of the storm in this harbor."

Irdek contained his questions until they had finished the meal. But then he pressed for details. Allyn described their adventures in detail.

Irdek glanced at the somber faces around him. "Were there any other survivors?"

Allyn told of the nine hanging on the dinghy.

"I hope the monsters of the deep didn't get them." Jarell

exchanged a look with Allyn.

Giada shuddered beside him. "I thought we were going to die on the raft."

Somberly, Allyn squeezed her shoulder.

"All the more reason why you don't belong on this adventure, Giada. As soon as we make port, we should send you back to your family." Jarell gave her a tight-lipped stare.

But she faced him with a mulish expression. "Need I remind you that the One Who Fashioned All gave me the vision of the firebird. I'm the only one who can recognize the mountain from a distance."

Irdek glanced from one to another. "Lauryn told me you were on a quest for a bird."

"You spoke to Lauryn? Is she well?" Allyn saw the look of surprise cross Jarell's face, matching his own feelings.

"I thought you knew she came to the isles searching for it." Irdek looked puzzled. Something else lurked in his eyes. It looked suspiciously like shame or guilt. *Why hadn't he mentioned Lauryn's name until now?*

"We got separated at our journey's start. But you haven't said if she's safe." Allyn's muscles tensed. He removed his arm from Giada. *If Irdek let anything befall Lauryn...*

"She fell into the Pirate King's hands." Irdek spread his hands. "One of our elders betrayed us. Dahl will never cause trouble again." The fire in Irdek's eyes let Allyn know his tribe had dealt with the traitor. Probably dead. The Nyrmidions were swift and fierce in their justice. "And even now we sail to rescue your sister. Dahl gave us the location of his fortress after much—" he glanced at Giada and away, "persuasion."

"So what are we waiting for?" Jarell growled.

"Nothing. Now that the storm ended and we have provisions, we will be there in a few hours." Irdek gave a wolfish grin. "Captain Yeager and his band of cutthroats will reap our wrath."

Only then did the sensation of motion cause Allyn to realize that they were already underway, and had been for some time.

---

8 Storm

Things were even worse than before. Not only was Lauryn locked on the top floor in the pirate stronghold, but Everard and Xylander were imprisoned somewhere in the fortress, too. Probably in the dungeons, if there were any.

When the pirates recaptured her, they thoroughly searched her. Gone was her dirk. Being men, they didn't confiscate the hairpins hidden in her braid. They had also stripped her companions of their swords and daggers.

Their captors tied the young men's hands behind their backs and marched them all back in single file to the dinghy.

The captain met them as they were hauled aboard. He took Lauryn's chin in his hand. "You're a plucky one, doll. But there's no tricking Yeager. You may be a princess, but I'm the king of the pirates." His eyes glinted with malice as he leaned toward her. "You won't escape me again."

"Unhand her, you dog!" Everard tried to lunge forward. His eyes blazed and his jaw clenched. He desperately grappled against the two men holding him.

Tauntingly, Yeager ran a finger down Lauryn's cheek.

She flinched, and Everard doubled his efforts to throw off his captor with a growl. She had never seen him so angry. She had stupidly wished to see Ever discomposed. She'd gotten her wish.

The pirate king pushed Lauryn into a sailor's arms. He clasped her back against his chest. She struggled but his hands around her upper arms were like iron manacles.

Yeager approached Everard, staring at him with a calculating gleam. "What have we here? A noble knight." The pirate king turned his gaze on Xylander, who returned it with fire in his eyes. "And a beardless youth." He guffawed, ignoring Xylander's hiss. He swung back to Lauryn. "Not much of a rescue launched on your behalf. princess. I expected your family to send a platoon, at the least."

He stroked his beard. "Maybe your mother will pay for them too. Or maybe they'll be shark bait. Time will tell."

Lauryn lifted her chin. "We are friends to the Nyrmidion people. We have trade agreements between—"

He cut her off. "You'd be surprised to know that not all our people are enamored of your mother or her God." He spat. "That's why my cousin Dahl alerted me to your presence. Pirating pays better than raising coconuts and bananas and selling them to your country."

Lauryn recalled how Dahl had spat when he said Everard had showed up at the sacred sight, the old pagan altar. So, he was the traitor in Irdek's village who alerted Yeager to her presence.

Under the captain's orders, the pirates escorted them into the cargo hold where they were kept under key the whole time. There was no use trying to escape. Even if they could, jumping into the water would be foolhardy.

As a pirate hoisted Lauryn from the dinghy, she had a chance to see her prison from the outside. When she first arrived, she had been drugged. And when she escaped, she never looked back.

Now she saw the sprawling stone edifice, four stories tall, crowned with a great slate roof punctuated with chimneys. Marks were left from vines that once covered the walls. Of course, the pirates wouldn't want to leave prisoners any access for climbing.

Isolated, it stood on a rocky promontory jutting into the sea. A cluster of huts crouched on the edge of the jungle.

The harbor was big and deep enough to anchor a fleet of ships, though only the pirate vessel rode there.

She wondered if knights had built the castle fortress as a defense. It had the look of an ancient stronghold.

Despair clutched her in its grip. The fortress seemed impregnable.

Once again wearing a manacle bracelet, Lauryn sat slumped against the wall. The taste of freedom made her continued captivity all the more galling. What hope had she now? What use was unlocking her manacles when she was forty feet above the ground?

Tap. Tap-tap. Tap.

Great. All she needed was rats running around the place. Lauryn hunched her shoulders even more.

Hope.

Ransom will be paid.

Wait! Those weren't her thoughts. The tapping was a message! Her mind had subconsciously decoded it. She recognized the code she and Allyn had come up with as children. *Was Allyn here? Had he come to rescue her?*

Her heart rate picked up. She jumped to her feet and raced as close as she could to the window. Through a knothole in the shutters, she saw the sun was setting. A dark mass of clouds reflected pink and orange. A storm was coming in tonight. But no other ship other than the pirates' was anchored in the harbor.

Answer if hear me.

And then Lauryn knew. Everard! He and Allyn had used their code on their capers.

She was disappointed that it wasn't her twin. Yet it was sweet of Everard to worry about her and try to reassure her. He reminded her that she wasn't in this alone. Father had sent him since he couldn't come himself.

And, of course, the One Who Fashioned All was aware of her plight.

She traced the tapping sound to the wall on her right.

She should buck up and try to come up with a plan. She

wasn't facing death, only temporary imprisonment. She mustn't despair, but hope.

She picked up her tin cup. She searched her memory for the letter code. She'd keep it simple. She used the cup to tap out a message. *Thanks, Ev. Better, knowing you nearby.*

And she was. She would still look for an opportunity to escape, but she knew that he would as well.

Sleep well, Laurie. She hadn't heard that nickname in a long, long time.

And you. It gave her comfort knowing that only a wall separated her from him.

She eventually drifted off to sleep. A loud noise awakened her, repeated over and over. She sat up and rubbed her arms in the coolness. Wind slapped the shutters. A draft of cool air whistled through the knothole. The storm must be upon them.

She reasoned they could use this storm to their advantage. No one in their right mind would try to escape during the wild weather. Any sounds she made would be indistinguishable in the noise.

Lauryn removed a hairpin and made quick work of her manacle. The hairpin wouldn't be any use on the door. When they shoved her in here, she had seen the wooden bar outside her door and heard her captors lower it in place.

That only left the window. She couldn't scale down the wall forty feet, but she could possibly climb over to Everard's window.

Feeling the crack between shutters, Lauryn touched the iron hasp holding them in place. As she loosened it, the wind grabbed it from her hands and slammed the left shutter onto the outer wall. Fortunately, the noise was lost in the storm's wild wailing. She pushed the right shutter over. It listed to one side, then dropped away. At least one barrier between her and the next window was gone.

Lauryn stuck her head out, gauging the distance. Only a few feet separated the windows. A two-inch ledge ran the length of the side. The wall was pitted and craggy—plenty of holds for fingers and toes. It would be fairly easy in dry weather. But the wet slickness and wind would be a challenge.

The shutter nearest her was crooked; the pair rattled with every blast of wind. Probably as weak as hers. She'd hope.

She pulled back into the room. In those few seconds, the rain had drenched her hair and ran in rivulets down her face.

She would wait until the storm died down before attempting to climb across from her prison to Everard's.

In preparation, she pinned her braid more securely.

After several hours of fitful sleep, she realized that the storm had lost intensity.

She sat down and removed her boots, tying the laces together. She stuffed her socks in them and slung the laces over her shoulders. Thank the Creator she had worn her leather dress that fell a few inches below her knees, rather than a court gown on this trip.

She knelt for a moment in the shelter of the room and prayed for success. *Please keep me safe. Let this escape work. Not only for me and my companions, but for the good of Valdeor.*

Afraid she would lose her courage if she lingered any longer, Lauryn climbed out the window. Without protection, the rain sliced at her like pebble projectiles. She concentrated only on the wall in front of her. She felt with her fingers for holds. Her bare feet slid along the ledge. Going was slippery, so she took her time. The cold water sluiced down the back of her neck. She was drenched in minutes.

When she was beside the next-door room's shutter, she reached with her left arm and yanked at it. She felt it give. Taking a deep breath, her feet curled with the effort to cling to the narrow ledge, she grasped the corner of the wood and pulled again. The shutter flew past her head, yanked away by a sudden gust. It glanced off her left shoulder, nearly making her lose her grip.

Her strength ebbing, she carefully positioned herself beside the window. With a mighty effort, she grabbed the sill and pulled herself through. She landed in an inelegant heap on the floor. Even though the rain pelted through the open window, the room was calm compared to the waning force of the storm outside.

"Lauryn?" Everard's voice came from the darkness. "Lauryn! Are you all right?"

A thrill shivered up her spine. She'd made it!

She knelt, using her hands to push wet strands of her hair out of her face. Getting to her feet, she stumbled toward the sound of Everard's voice.

"Lauryn! What were you thinking? You might've fallen. You might've died!" From the torchlight in the room, she could see Everard's angry glare. Behind his tone, she could sense his fear for her.

"I didn't think a girl could do that." Xylander's voice was filled with astonishment. "And in this tempest!"

"I'm fine. I think I was fourteen when you taught me to climb, that summer we visited Winterhome." Lauryn glanced at Everard.

She sat beside him and worked on unlacing her boots. It was hard going. Her hands were icy from exposure. Everard put his warm hand over hers to stop her. Reproaching her as he worked, he unknotted the wet laces.

"That was the foolhardiest thing you have ever done! And you've done some pretty stupid things. I should know. I was there for many of them," Everard chided her, even while handing the boots over. "I taught Allyn to climb. You only tagged along."

"Are you done? Do you want me to release your hands or not? I can always go back to my solitary prison if you don't want my help." She knew she sounded petulant, but if he had done the same to reach her, he'd expect her to praise him.

As if he read her thoughts, Everard sighed. "I value your life more than that. What would I do if anything happened to you?"

His words mollified her, until he added, "—under my watch. How could I answer to your father"

Wounded by his unfeeling words, she ground out, "If it's only your reputation you're worried about, I'm sure Xylander would be happy to accompany me for the rest of the journey. Without you." She turned away from him angrily and went to kneel in front of Xylander. She used her hairpin to unlock his manacle first.

Why, oh why, did she let Everard get under her skin?

"I think I vastly underestimated you." Xylander stood when she freed him. He reached down and pulled her to her feet. His hand was firm and warm.

"Maybe a biddable wife isn't as important to have as a resourceful one." He tilted his head to look at her as if genuinely puzzled. "I find your courage...intoxicating."

Lauryn pulled her hand from his and stepped back. She didn't know whether to feel flattered, or as if she were a cow up for sale, as he cataloged her good points.

She searched his face expecting to see a sneer, yet his eyes said he was in earnest. His genuine admiration made him more handsome.

She had a sudden, burning desire to know why he had joined her on this quest.

Xylander confused her.

"Don't encourage her." Ever said in a dry voice.

Ever sighed, and she turned toward the sound. He was standing, his bound hands held out in front of him. "Kiss and make up, Laurie. I didn't mean to hurt your feelings. You are beautiful and brave, as Xylander says. But you scared me to death."

She could see the sincerity written on his face.

She caught Xylander's horrified look at the beginning of Ever's apology. She chuckled. "He isn't going to kiss me. It's a phrase. It means 'forgive and forget.'"

Everard grinned, sheepishly. "You know I couldn't live without your cutting remarks. Or the twinkle in your fiery eyes." His familiar teasing washed away her irritation with him. "Free me, like a good girl."

She huffed for effect, letting him know he wasn't entirely off the hook. *The things she would do for one of Ever's rare smiles.* She crossed over and unlocked his manacles. He immediately rubbed his hands up and down her wet, cold arms. She shivered.

"You're freezing." Everard put his arm around her and pulled her close. He rubbed his other hand up and down her back. She melted a little and rested her forehead on his chest for a moment.

Xylander made a disparaging sound. "Don't kiss in my presence!" Then he walked to the door and yanked on it without success.

A strange desire for Ever to do just that passed over Lauryn. His touch was comforting.

When Everard brushed her bruised left shoulder, Lauryn winced. She stepped away from the embrace, pushing down the attraction for her old crush.

Everard picked up on her grimace. "What is it? Are you hurt?"

She shrugged, unwisely, and bit back a groan. "The shutter hit me as it flew away. It's nothing."

He frowned. She forestalled him when he would speak, turning to watch Xylander. "It's barred on the outside."

Xylander growled and put his shoulder into it before giving up.

She glanced between them and they stared back at her, at a loss for a solution. "I did my part. Getting through that door takes brawn. Now it's over to you men."

"As in we're the muscle and you're the brains?" Everard challenged her.

He strode toward her, his face determined. He went past her and grabbed the remaining shutter. He wrenched the iron hasp from the rotting wood. Approaching the door, he inserted the hasp in the gap between door and lintel. He worked it into the space, then he lifted it up. He pushed it up until he caught the bar on the other side. With a sudden crash, the bar slipped with a clang outside the door.

"Nothing to it, my dear." He grinned at Lauryn who gaped at him. Then he relented. "Actually, I worked that solution out hours ago. But without you freeing us from the chains, it did no good. So, we're even." He put a friendly hand on her good shoulder.

Warmth filled her chest at his acknowledgment.

While they talked, Xylander eagerly pushed past them. He checked to see that no one was outside, then he stalked out. But when Lauryn was ready to follow, Ever pushed in front of her.

"Too dangerous. I'll go first."

Xylander, waiting in the hall, hushed them. "Now, let us find some swords." Lauryn could swear he purred as he said it.

The trio went through a series of hallways until they found a narrow staircase along the fortress's outer wall. Deep window wells, placed at regular intervals, were for shooting arrows or pouring hot oil on enemy forces. They felt their way down the dimly lit, damp stairwell when the sound of many boots heading their way made them pause.

Everard, still behind Lauryn, grabbed her and pushed her back the way they came. He whispered a plan in her ear. "Up! Hurry!" To Xylander, he hissed, "Flatten yourself in one of the alcoves."

As she passed him, Everard wedged himself into a dark space.

She went a little further and stopped before a bend in

the stairs. When the first man came into sight, she let out a scream. Making eye contact with him, she spun and rounded the corner. Hopefully the pirates wouldn't see her friends hiding as they focused on her. She didn't go very far before she heard a scuffle behind her. Cries and shouts sounded, and the ring of steel on steel.

Lauryn crept back to the corner and looked down. Everard and Xylander had swords in one hand, daggers in the other, and bodies at their feet. The narrow space meant only one pirate at a time could approach. Whoever got past Xylander, Everard struck down.

After Xylander dispatched the last man with a kick that sent him flying back down the stairs, Everard turned and saw her. He reached down and extricated a dagger from the nearest opponent's body.

As he reached her side, he handed it over. "Good job distracting them." *Was that approval in his eyes?* She tucked the weapon in her belt.

"I think the party is heading up this way." Everard took her arm and they jogged back up the stairs.

"But we'll get trapped!" Xylander protested behind them.

"I thought I saw an outer staircase from the ship's deck. If we can find that, we can avoid the main areas." Everard seemed sure of himself.

They soon came to a dead end, a short flight up from where they started. A heavy wooden door blocked their way.

Xylander faced the way they came while Everard tried the door latch. When it didn't move, he glanced down at Lauryn. "Over to you and your lock picks." He moved to the side.

The cramped area gave little room to work. She brushed past Everard. He stood so close she could feel his breath on the back of her neck as he stood a few steps below her. Her heart rate picked up, whether at his nearness or the sense of urgency, she didn't try to analyze.

The keyhole was too large for a hairpin. She drew the stolen dagger but the blunt end wouldn't work. She needed a sharp point.

"Ever, let me borrow your dagger." She knew he would have loaded up with weapons from their enemies. Sure enough, he passed her a one with a fine point.

Her fingers fumbled as she tried to access the tumbler.

"You can do this, Lauryn." His confidence in her ability spread warmth through her insides. He might be dictatorial at times, but Everard was showing he could also be encouraging when she doubted herself.

She took a steadying breath. She wiggled the point around and heard a click.

"That's my girl." Everard reached past her with his arm, and pushed the heavy door open. Just in time, as shouts sounded from below.

Someone must've discovered the bodies on the stairwell!

The door opened into a tower. Lauryn rushed into the

room, Everard behind her. The round room was a dead end.

"Time to leave this vermin's nest!" Xylander cried.

"The window!" Everard approached the open space which looked out on the slate roof. He climbed out, as agile as a cat. Turning back, he held out his hand to Lauryn. She took it. His grasp was firm and strong. She stepped on the slanted roof. About twelve feet above their heads, it flattened out.

She realized two things. Everard had a gash on the arm holding her. Blood dripped from it. Secondly, it no longer rained heavily. The winds had died down since she climbed from her prison. A gust brought a sprinkle of rain, but the worst of the tempest seemed to be over.

Dropping Everard's hand, Lauryn knelt on the slanted roof line. She reached for handholds with her fingers. Unfortunately, she found very little to grab onto. Xylander swarmed past her like a monkey, finding toeholds seemingly out of the air.

Everard had also managed to scramble part way up. He leaned toward her and called, "Grab my hand, Laurie!"

She reached for it, and he grasped her right wrist. He hauled her up, awing her with his sheer strength. Shouts from below gave her a boost of nervous energy. Her feet somehow found purchase. Everard made it the rest of the way up, tugging her along with him. Reaching for the parapet, she held on with her left hand, feeling the strain in her injured shoulder. It passed quickly as Everard pulled her to safety on the flat roof.

They scrambled behind a chimney stack and stopped to catch their breath.

"Let me see your gash." Lauryn insisted on tearing a fabric strip from Everard's tunic hem and wrapping it around his injured arm.

"It's only a surface scratch." Everard kept an eye on the tower.

"Here they come!" Xylander flattened himself along the chimney. When the first man hauled himself over the parapet, Xylander sprang on him. Slashing him, he sent the pirate hurtling to the ground below.

"Hide!" Everard commanded her before he joined the prince in defending the rooftop.

Knowing she was no match for the intense sword fight, Lauryn ran from chimney to chimney, staying out of sight. Reaching the roof's opposite corner, she leaned over, searching for the stair that Everard claimed he had seen. The tower on the east end had its roof missing. Vines wrapped around it, possibly offering a way down. She tugged on one as thick as her wrist. It held securely in place.

A noise behind her made her turn her head. The pirate king climbed onto the roof. Her movement caught his eye. She bolted toward the nearest chimney stack. Getting it between her and her pursuer, she angled off in a different direction and ran.

Crouching behind a broken pile of masonry, she peeked

around it, looking for Yeager. Her hand rested on a rough stone, giving her an idea. She picked it up and threw it toward the far side of the roof. Captain Yeager paused, then headed toward the sound.

Lauryn raced for another tower. Leaning over the parapet, she saw stairs circling the tower's outer wall.

A cry below her caused her to glance outward. She froze at the sight before her. A second ship rode in the harbor. Men fiercely battled on the beach. She thought she saw Marjek's red horns on a tall warrior, swinging a mighty blade.

Surely that must be Allyn fighting nearby. She'd recognize her twin anywhere. And that meant the tigerish fighter at his back was Jarell. *Help had come!* She let out a glad cry.

A scraping sound warned Lauryn of danger. Swinging about, dagger in her hand, she deflected Captain Yeager's falling blow. She had momentarily forgotten him.

The wind whipped wisps of her braid around her face, but she couldn't push them away.

A kerchief mostly covered his greasy hair, keeping it out of his eyes. His black eyes taunted her as he pressed her with a wicked-looking, curved dagger. "So, you are a warrior princess?"

He wasted no more words, but his smirk spoke volumes. Quick breaths and grunts sounded as he rained jabbing blows with his weapon that beat in time with Lauryn's rapid pulse. He pushed her back toward the tower wall. He might have brute strength, but she used her agility. She danced under, and twisted away, from his thrusts. But he had the advantage, and they both knew it.

She would have to end this before he wore her out. Keeping her eye on him, trying to predict each move, meant she couldn't assess the area for an escape route. She contemplated a dangerous idea: leap over the side where the tower joined the roof, and hope she landed safely on the stairs below.

9 Reunion

*A*llyn ferociously attacked a pirate. Jarell fought at his back. Already, the shore was littered with bodies from both sides. Sweat dripped down Allyn's face, but he didn't have time to wipe it away.

They had sailed into the harbor on the tail end of the storm. Irdek's forces had met the fortress's pirates in a mighty clash as they streamed onto the beach.

Now, after an intense forty-five-minute battle, the enemy was dwindling.

Dispatching his foe, he stalked forward to meet the next pirate. A feint, a lunge, then he thrust the Crestin sword into the man's gut. Glancing around, he realized the pitched battle was over.

Irdek, wearing his father's red horns, lifted his sword and shouted a guttural cry of victory. His men lifted their swords and shouted the same. Allyn and Jarell wiped their swords, sheathed them, and joined Irdek at the fortress forecourt.

The heavy wooden door swung open and Lauryn burst out. She threw her arms around Allyn, nearly knocking him over in her exuberance.

"Allyn! Thank the Creator you're here!" She strangled him and he crushed her back.

"When Irdek said you'd been captured, I was out of my mind with worry." Allyn pulled back to look down at her. "Is everything all right with you? Has Xylander been a gentleman?" He lifted his eyes and stared at the young prince standing in the doorway. Xylander glared right back at him.

"I'm fine." But she winced when Jarell grabbed her shoulders in a hug.

Before Allyn could ask any more questions, Lauryn took charge.

"Thank you for coming, Irdek. We have the pirate king subdued inside." She put her hands on her hips. "My friends wanted to dispatch him, but I thought doling out justice belonged to you."

Irdek promised that he and his father would mete out justice according to their laws. For now, he would see Yeager imprisoned in the dungeon until they were ready to sail, then transfer him to the brig. He directed the rest of his men to deal with the dead and wounded.

Lauryn led Allyn, Jarell, and Irdek inside.

They entered into the great room, which was half the size of the throne room back home. The remnants of a hastily left meal littered two giant trestle tables. Against one stone wall stood a giant fireplace. Crossed pikes and other weapons decorated the walls.

In front of it, a man was tied up while a familiar man guarded him.

Irdek dealt with the prisoner, while Allyn blinked at the sight of his good friend. "Everard!"

Hearing his name uttered, Everard looked up and met Allyn's gaze. His frown changed into a grin. He strode over and they clasped each other's shoulders.

"Ev! What are you doing here?" Allyn's spirit soared knowing another stalwart friend had joined their ranks. Everard might be taciturn, but there was no one he'd rather have at his back than the quiet prince.

"Father sent him to babysit me, that's what." Lauryn elbowed Everard. Her voice was dry but Allyn could tell she wasn't upset. Well, not too upset.

The two of them had always had a prickly relationship. Lauryn was independent, so Everard's natural tendency to protect irked her. And Everard tended to be frank in his opinions, ruffling Lauryn's feathers. She had a crush on Everard as a teen. That had seemed to make Everard uncomfortable—although he never acknowledged out loud that he even knew of it.

Allyn wondered how Everard and Lauryn had managed to get along while journeying together these many weeks without his buffering presence.

"Good thing your father sent me, else this blackguard, Yeager, would still have you at his mercy." Everard glanced down at Lauryn.

"I had a plan to escape him but you came before I could execute it." She crossed her arms.

"Jumping from the slate roof to the winding tower stairs is not a plan. It's suicide." Everard looked exasperated.

Glancing between them, Allyn demanded an explanation. He was glad to know Everard had arrived in time and disarmed the pirate before he harmed Lauryn.

"It sounds to me like Everard has had his hands full with taking care of you, Lauryn." He frowned at his sister but she only jutted her chin out.

"You would take his side," she huffed. "Have Everard tell you how I rescued him first."

Everard retorted, "With an equally risky move. You forget how important a person you are. Your countrymen depend on you. You may be chosen the next ruler, if only you can show some common sense." He frowned at her.

A commotion behind him had Allyn turning around. Giada was arguing with Irdek's men, demanding to be let in. Mystic cautiously sniffed the men's boots. Talk about having one's hands full...

"Giada! You're safe!" Lauryn caught sight of her friend and held out her arms.

Giada rushed into her hug and burst into tears, even though the danger had passed. Girls were confusing.

Jarell rolled his eyes beside Allyn.

Giada wiped away her tears, trying to compose herself.

Xylander stared, looking her over from her cut hair to

her boy's leggings. Her boyish appearance seemed to shock him. "Giada, why did you come?" His voice and expression were stern, raising Allyn's hackles. "Your father will be furious. You should have stayed home where you belong, cousin."

This unwise speech caused Giada to break into fresh tears.

Allyn clenched his teeth. *Did the prince have no tact?*

"Why are you upset?" Glancing from her to Allyn and Jarell, Xylander barked, "Did the brothers hurt you?"

Fury surged through Allyn. "How dare you! We took excellent care of her, as if she were our own sister." He gripped his sword's hilt. "What right do you have to tell her what to do, anyway?"

The young prince's nostrils flared and anger flashed in his eyes. "I have every right. She is my fiancé."

Allyn pulled up short. A spurt of jealousy flared in him. Glancing at Giada he saw her equally stunned expression. Allyn frowned. Something was off.

His gut seethed. "Well, I don't like you traveling with my sister."

"You dare question my honor?" The younger man whipped out his scimitar and advanced on Allyn.

"You impugned mine!" In defense, Allyn unsheathed the Crestin sword.

They came to blows before a third sword pressed their locked blades down. "Enough!" Everard looked mad enough to spit nails.

Lauryn and Giada stared at them with pale faces.

Jarell said, "It wasn't our idea to take Giada along. In fact, we tried to send her home."

Heat crept up Allyn's neck. His anger had overcome his good sense. No matter how irritating the younger prince was, he should act the adult. If his goal was to prove he was fit to become high king, he should control his emotions.

Lauryn thrust herself between the two combatants. Everard had stopped them physically, but she used her diplomatic skills.

"We are royals! Let us act like it and conduct our business like civilized people." She glared from one to the other.

Allyn seemed ashamed of giving into his temper. She wondered how much of that was due to his obvious feelings for Giada. She had seen the shock and hurt when Xylander announced his so-called betrothal.

As for the Canteor prince, his pride and temper were still on display.

Swallowing her own pride, Lauryn lightly touched his arm. "I trust my brother's word. Similarly, as you acted like a gentleman on our travels, he would do the same."

Mollified, Xylander put away his scimitar.

She gestured. "Some food would do us good and help

our tempers. I am sure we all want to hear each other's stories."

The pirates must've been sitting down to a meal when the alarm was raised at their escape earlier. Beside the two long trestle tables, a side table was piled high with meat on platters, bread loaves, and local fruits and nuts.

She motioned for everyone to help themselves to the feast.

They cleared off one table. Giada sat on one side of Lauryn and Everard sat on her other. Jarell was across from them. Xylander staked out his place on Giada's other side. A quick flash of irritation crossed Allyn's face as he took his seat, then he put on his court mask.

Knowing that Xylander would be the least patient, desiring to hear about Giada, she motioned for Allyn to report on their wanderings first.

She squeezed Giada's hand at hearing about the fight in the alleyway. She stared at the jagwaro purring in Giada's lap that she had taken for a full-grown house cat. She gasped at the avalanche and giant salamander.

Lauryn put down her fork. "One day, about three weeks into our quest, I felt dizzy. I thought you were in trouble since I had no reason to feel sick."

Allyn squinted as he worked out the days. "The timing is right. That is the day the salamander bit and poisoned me."

When Allyn finished speaking, Lauryn filled the others in on her and her companions' adventures. She ended with the fight on the roof.

It seemed that the sight of Irdek's ship had drawn away most of the pirates, allowing Xylander and Everard to go in search of her. Before she had a chance to execute her risky plan, Xylander had tackled the pirate king, and Ever had disarmed him.

"So what happens next?" Allyn pushed away his empty plate.

Everard was staring at the table. Giada looked ready to fall asleep. Jarell had wandered away and was gazing at the displayed weaponry.

Xylander glanced proudly at the others. "I know where the firebird is. I've known since the beginning."

"What?!" Jarell exploded. He crossed the room in quick strides, putting his hands on his hips and glaring at the prince. "Why didn't you say so? Why let us nearly die?" He looked ready to punch Xylander.

"It is my privilege as crown prince to know. The firebird, found only in Canteor, is the symbol of our strength and might." He crossed his arms, his expression scornful. "I don't know why foreigners were given the task to find it."

Dismay filled Lauryn to the core. "You as good as promised you would help me find it back when we killed the boar. Will you back out of your agreement now?"

Xylander sent her a stubborn glare.

"If he won't help you, I will." Giada sat up straight. She looked different, and it wasn't only due to the boy's clothes and shoulder-length hair. She wasn't the shy, quiet girl Lauryn once knew. Giada wore a dagger tucked in her belt. Her eyes and posture held boldness.

"You?" Xylander's eyes widened.

"I saw the firebird in a vision. You're not the only one who can guide them. The One Who Fashioned All gave me the knowledge, too." Confidence—that's what she had.

"The clues have gotten us this far. I vote we trust Giada's vision." Everard crossed his arms on the table beside Lauryn, who leaned forward in her chair. "But this is your quest." Everard quirked an eyebrow at her.

Warmth filled her as he deferred to her. Maybe he was finally realizing she was no longer a child for him to boss around. She might one day be his queen.

Her heart stumbled at the thought. *Queen of his realm. Not queen of his heart. She'd never win his heart. Did she still want to?*

She realized everyone was looking at her. Heat crawled up her neck and face as she tried to focus. What had Everard said? "Um, yes, I vote we sail to Canteor so Giada can find the firebird's home."

They talked further, but the thing they all needed most was sleep. "We can discuss it tomorrow." Lauryn's bones were like wax after the climb and the fight. She absently rubbed her shoulder where the shutter had hit her.

Irdek joined them with the news that he and his men had swept the fortress. All the surviving pirates were in the dungeon with their leader.

Allyn led the way upstairs. Both he and Xylander offered their arms to a yawning Giada. They glared at each other over her head. Instead of choosing between them, Giada clung to Lauryn. They found two rooms side by side—a smaller room for the girls and a bigger one for the boys. Everard checked the latch on the girls' window, while Lauryn yanked the dirty bedding off the cots.

"Yell if you need us." Allyn gave her a hug before he left. "It's good to be together again."

"I'll take first watch" Jarell sat down on the floor between the rooms.

"You don't trust Irdek and his men?" Xylander glanced down the hall.

"At this point, I don't trust anyone but my brother and Everard." Jarell glared at the Canteoran.

Xylander thrust his nose in the air and stomped into the boys' room, Allyn and Everard following him.

Lauryn closed the door behind them. Giada looked as if she were already asleep, curled up on her cot. Lauryn wrapped herself in her cloak and lay on the other one.

She was thankful for her brothers' presence. Her confidence soared now that the original group was together again. Relaxing for the first time in weeks, she drifted off to sleep.

The next afternoon, they sailed away from the pirate outpost. Irdek had cut his forces in half. Some men took the pirates and their ship back to Marjek's isle. Irdek and his hand-picked crew had agreed to take Lauryn, her brothers, and the other royals the rest of the way to Canteor aboard the *Valiant*.

The days at sea took on a rhythm of their own. Up at dawn to stretch and exercise. The boys practiced with swords. Allyn and Xylander seemed to have an unspoken agreement. They avoided crossing blades, fighting with Jarell or Everard by turns. The girls worked on defensive tactics with and without weapons. Hard tack for breakfast, washed down with tea, followed.

After that, Jarell would help the crew with their tasks. Allyn and Everard pored over maps and discussed strategy. They helped haul the fish nets aboard. Lauryn and Giada mended the sails ripped in the storm. Xylander mostly kept to himself.

On the fourth day at sea, Lauryn sparred with Giada, then praised her for how far she had come in her self-defense. The once-shy girl showed confidence and boldness in her moves.

They stood idly at the bulwark after the practice session.

"Allyn had me practice daily whenever possible. I resented it at first. But when I didn't think I could keep it up, the memory of those criminals in the alley flashed across my eyes."

"How awful! Do you want to talk about it?" Lauryn still woke up some mornings, afraid she was a prisoner aboard the pirate ship. How much worse was a glimpse of violence for Giada, whom her parents coddled to the point that she hardly knew of the wickedness of the world.

Shuddering, Giada told her about the men trapping her and Allyn in the alleyway. How helpless she had felt. How brave Allyn had been, protecting her. "I had nightmares for days afterward. I guess I am pampered, as Jarell says. I never worried about my safety before. Guards accompanied me whenever I left the palace." She wrapped her arms around her middle. "Allyn has been very kind and patient with me, spending hours on my self-defense." She blushed.

"I don't think it's disinterested kindness on his part." Lauryn fought back a grin. But she didn't elaborate at Giada's confused expression.

The weeks quickly passed. Then one afternoon, the sailor in the crow's nest called out, "Land!"

Lauryn dropped the fish net she was mending and hurried to the rails. Her companions soon gathered around her. She made out a smudge on the horizon.

Irdek left the wheelhouse and joined them. "We should find a harbor to land at tomorrow or the next day." He glanced at Xylander. "Since you are from here, where do you propose we go, Your Highness?"

"The western coast has many small fishing villages. The biggest harbor is three days sailing to Caervale. From there we can make our way up the Merione Mountains—the legendary firebird's home." A frown marred his handsome face as he straightened, fingering his scimitar's hilt. "Although, you realize, the bird may be a myth. No one has seen it in hundreds of years."

"I saw it," Giada piped up. Lauryn and the others turned to look at her. "It was in a vision, but it was so real."

Xylander grunted, wearing a look of disbelief. "The firebird is sacred to my people." Xylander huffed. "I should be the one to find it."

Giada bit her lip. "Doesn't the mirror pool show you the truth of your desire?"

Lauryn saw Allyn rub his leg absently at the mention of the mirror pool. She wondered if it was a reflexive action or did his poisoned bite still bother him. When he was tired, she'd noticed he limped, favoring the leg.

Surprisingly, Jarell defended Giada. "That is how Father found Mother. We know this to be true."

Giada's mouth opened with surprise. Jarell winked at her.

Glancing at Everard, Lauryn waited to see if he approved the plan.

Lauryn didn't trust Xylander. He blew hot and cold. First, he kept the whereabouts to himself. Then he agreed to help them, albeit reluctantly. Now he claimed they may be on a wild goose chase, or wild firebird chase, as it were.

Lauryn wondered if he had a hidden agenda of his own.

Why had he come on this journey? Originally Lauryn had thought Aunt Donella played at matchmaker. But maybe her honorary aunt had guessed that the prince knew the firebird's location.

Did he plan to snatch it, keeping the twins from their goal? He said it was an important symbol of power in his culture. Would he lead them to it?

How significant was plucking a feather from the firebird in their quest? Wasn't this a character test? A display of virtue? Would trusting Xylander prove a virtue? Or would prudence be better since he was an unknown factor? Was he an ally or an enemy?

With so many questions, Lauryn couldn't make up her mind. Everard seemed to be weighing the options, too.

Allyn glanced at Giada. "Is this where your vision sent you?"

She scrunched up her nose. "I only know that it's somewhere in Canteor. The firebird lives on a very distinctive mountain peak. I'd recognize it if I saw it."

Lauryn looked to her twin. Allyn stared off into the distance. Seeming to make up his mind, he glanced between Everard and Lauryn. "I vote we listen to Xylander. He does know this continent better than we do." Allyn's expression was resigned, as if he didn't want to agree with the Canteor prince.

Xylander wore a superior smile.

Lauryn saw her brother's jaw tighten. He mightn't like

the other prince, but he wouldn't let that stop him from doing the right thing. Lauryn admired her twin for that.

Everard and Jarell agreed with Allyn. Lauryn's vote didn't hold much weight now that the others had decided their course of action. She nodded anyway. Let the decision rest on everyone else. She had a bad feeling about this.

10 Allyria and Allek

The rain fell in heavy sheets in the weeks after the eldest twins and Jarell left. The dreariness of the days and silence with half of her siblings gone grated on Allyria. Even sitting in her favorite reading spot, a window seat, with an adventure story in her hands, couldn't chase away her blue mood. Normally placid, an uncharacteristic desire for action burned within her. There must be something she could do.

Being twelve meant she and her twin were aware of the situation and wanted to help Mother, yet the grown-ups kept them in the dark, as if they were little children.

Allyria knew Allek felt their inaction even keener than she did. He wanted their parents to treat him as they did the older boys. Allek loved to play pranks and goad his elders, but that was the form his restless energy took.

Many of the things he did were clever.

Allek hid himself in the secret room off of the throne room, meant to hide guards during tense diplomatic meetings, every time a courier brought news.

That is how the twins knew of the pirate king's ransom

note demanding money for Lauryn's safe return.

So, Allyria wasn't surprised when Mr. Savon, Allek's tutor, escorted her brother precipitately into the library, a stack of reading material in his arms ready to topple over.

"Take an example from your dear sister and apply yourself to your studies, young master. I would hate to have to go to your father and complain about your behavior when your mother's illness already presses on him." Mr. Savon spoke in a high, displeased voice and wrung his hands before shutting the door on Allek.

Allyria looked to her twin. "What have you done, now?" she questioned, curious rather than accusatory.

Allek let the books haphazardly slide on the central library table where not long ago they had excitedly pored over the books of myth and lore. Now their elder siblings were hunting down the legendary firebird while the younger twins did their lessons.

Even though she was supposed to be studying, she rebelled. *High Seas* might sound like a geography book, but was actually a story about pirates.

"It's what I haven't done that I'm in trouble for." Allek removed a slingshot from his pocket and proceeded to shoot peanuts into the enormous marble fireplace.

"I told you I'd help you study for the mathematics test." Allyria closed her book with a snap.

"There must be something we can do to help Mother." Allyria kicked her heels against the wood wainscot. "If

Lauryn and Allyn need to prove which one is worthy for the crown, then Mother must be worse off than we think."

Having run out of peanuts, Allek slumped sideways on a plush chair. "Like what? We aren't healers. Even your book learning cannot compete against the royal physicians' recommendations. They've tried everything." He scrunched up his nose. "Lysa, at age six, is happy to fetch and carry for Mother. I don't have her patience. And don't lecture me that doing my schoolwork well is most pleasing to Mother, like Mr. Savon tells me. Daily."

"I've been thinking." Allyria laid down the book on the seat and walked around the room, her fingers lightly touching the books on the shelves. "The physicians have tried every remedy and herb and concoction. But they haven't tried one thing."

Allek stretched and tried doing a handstand against the back of the chair. Father should really let him train more on the practice field. Allek really needed a physical outlet. Allyria made a mental note to bring it up at supper.

Stopping next to Allek's chair, she stared at his upside-down face. "The elixir of the water of regeneration."

"What!" Allek tumbled gracefully into a crouch. "You mean, you're suggesting we should travel to the mysterious Isle of Origin?"

She nodded, even as fear twisted her stomach at the thought.

Allek suddenly reached for her and felt her forehead.

"You are feeling well, aren't you? It isn't like you to want to go jaunting on an adventure, outside of your books."

Huffing, she pulled away. Fear for Mother outweighed her anxiety of traveling so far with only her twin for protection. "I don't want Mother to die. It's worth the risk of a scolding. Besides, pilgrims travel there all the time. Or, they used to." She bit her lip. "I heard Uncle Guy tell Aunt Donella he would head back to the Isle of Origin after sending Lauryn, Allyn and Jarell overseas. So, we'll be safe with him there."

"But we have no rings to travel through the portals." Standing, Allek rubbed his hand through his already mussed hair. "And Brodyn never takes his ring off, so I can't pinch it." Brodyn, the resident Waykeeper assigned to the capital city of Mintala, helped the portal travelers to and from the palace.

Allyria straightened the pile of books Allek had scattered on the table.

"Spill it, Allyria. You know a way or you wouldn't have brought it up."

"There's one who can travel at will through the portals without a ring." When her brother stared at her, she glanced at Allek under her lashes. "Have you visited the stables lately?"

He frowned. Then his face brightened as he connected her hints. "Seeker! He can carry the two of us through the portals!" The stallion was unique because he alone carried a brand on his flank with the portal symbol of interlocking ovals. He could walk through a portal to any place that his rider imagined.

Allyria dimpled. "Then you'll join me?"

"Of course!" Allek grabbed her upper arms, a huge grin on his face. That's as close as he would come to giving her a hug.

"Brilliant!" For him, that was the highest praise. "When do we leave?"

She grinned back. She never doubted that he would want to accompany her. "The day after tomorrow? That gives us time to save food from each meal."

Over the next days, they surreptitiously swiped rolls and fruit from the meals and snacks.

Allek strolled to the stables, and reported to Allyria that he had managed to hide a saddle and bridle under the straw.

On the chosen day, Allyria dressed in a plain, traveling gown. Retrieving the satchel hidden under her bed, she hefted it and sneaked out of her bedroom. It was early enough that her maid hadn't come and lit the fire yet.

She silently made her way into Lauryn's bedroom down the hall. Allek waited for her beside Lauryn's empty hearth.

"Why does Lauryn get a secret passage door in her room?" Allek whispered.

"Because Mother nor Father would ever trust you to have one. You already get into enough scrapes as it is. Besides, she is the crown princess. She needs an escape route if the palace were under attack." While she spoke, her fingers felt for the rose on the fireplace surround that opened the hidden entrance. Pushing on the correct one, a gap appeared on one side.

The twins slipped inside the dark passage. Allek lit the torch placed there for emergencies. They traveled through the stone passageway, pushing through cobwebs. They had thoroughly explored the hidden halls when much younger, known only to the royals and a few trusted guards. They avoided the dead-end tunnels with traps their ancestors put there against intruders.

In a short while, they ended up in the old well house, one of three exits.

They quickly made their way to the stable. Inside, Allyria fed Seeker a carrot she had snitched from the kitchen. Once Allek had saddled the stallion, and put his pack and Allyria's into the saddlebags, he mounted. Allyria climbed the stall enclosure. Allek reached over and pulled Allyria up behind him.

Her heart sped up. There was no going back now.

Allek nudged the stallion into motion, and Seeker sprinted into the palace courtyard. Several guards looked up as they burst onto the scene. Ignoring the shouts, Allek spurred the horse toward the garden gate separating the courtyard from the vegetable garden.

One garden post was made of wood and the other of stone. The interlocking ovals were etched in the stone post.

"Capall!" Allek shouted as they neared it. Mist rose up,

swirling into a circle. Through it appeared the town.

As the nearest guard reached out his hand to grab the bridle, Seeker leaped through the portal.

Allyria tightened her hold around her brother's waist as darkness and stars spun around them. As dizziness enveloped her, she almost regretted talking Allek into doing this. Unlike her siblings, she wasn't cut out for adventures. She preferred reading about them.

They emerged from the tunnel into Valdeor's busy horse-trading center. They were in front of Capall's biggest inn, the postern actually a portal. A few people scattered out of the way with sour looks, while others looked askance at the two youths.

Allek slipped off Seeker's back. He led the horse to the stable, Allyria still mounted.

"Where are you taking us, Allek? Shouldn't you ask the innkeeper the next stop on the route?" She glanced back at the inn.

"I thought we could explore the town."

"I don't think that's a good idea. Remember how Uncle Guy almost lost Seeker in this very town when buyers thought he was too young to own such a valuable animal? The same could happen to us!"

Allek paused and she knew he'd listen.

He sighed, changed direction, and led Seeker to the

164

water trough. "Stay here. Don't let anyone take him from you."

She promised to be vigilant. He strode across the yard and entered the inn door in search of information.

Allyria gazed around. The inn was located on the main thoroughfare. Traders rode along, with horses strung together trailing after them. Pedestrians strolled by, some stopping to comment on the horses, others hurrying about their business.

She garnered a few interested stares. Allyria clutched the reins tighter. This is exactly what she feared. She had no desire to expose herself as a royal, or explain how she came to be in possession of the extraordinary stallion.

Why hadn't she realized how vulnerable she and Allek would be?

Although Seeker was about twenty years old by her reckoning, he was still a fine steed. And their only means of transportation. What if someone tried to take him from her?

"Princess Allyria!" a familiar voice called out.

Turning in the saddle, she spotted Aunt Donella approaching.

Her heart sank at the thought that their adventure was about to come to an abrupt end.

She was tempted to kick Seeker into motion and hide in the town knowing Allek would seek her when he found her gone. But she squashed the temptation.

Aunt Donella's gaze landed on Seeker's brand, and her

eyes jumped back to Allyria's. "Do your parents know you're here alone?" Aunt Donella's hand reached over and grabbed the bridle.

Allyria sighed. No escape now.

"I'm not alone. I'm here with my brother." Allyria glanced back at the inn door. Where was Allek?

"Not your older brothers. They're across the Stormy Sea. If you mean your twin, he isn't enough to protect you. This is no place for a young princess."

As she watched, Allek surged out of the inn to stop short at the sight of Aunt Donella. Taking in the situation with a glance, he strode over.

Allyria tensed.

Allek met Allyria's glance and he deflated. Busted!

"Hello, Aunt Donella. We can explain—," Allek began.

"Not here. Let's go inside, where we can't be overheard. We don't want anyone recognizing the two of you." Aunt Donella called a groom over to take care of Seeker.

"Really, Allek," Aunt Donella scolded him after escorting the twins to her private parlor in the inn. "I'd expect such shenanigans from you. But to drag your sister along!"

No one said anything until the innkeeper's wife finished putting down a tray of tea and cakes, and took her leave.

"It wasn't his fault. I dragged him on my mission."

Aunt Donella's raised eyebrows said that she didn't believe Allyria.

"Truly I did." Allyria's impassioned voice warbled.

"We're tired of sitting around while Mother is dying. Then I remembered the holy well in the Isle of Origin and how many miraculous cures were obtained from the waters. The physicians don't think of things like that. Father has aged while the twins and Jarell have been gone. I—I figured no one would listen to us. So, I asked Allek to come along with me."

Allek spoke over a mouthful of cake, "Thaz wight. Couldn't let Awiya go 'lone."

Aunt Donella sighed and passed him a cup of lemonade. "I know you both want to do something useful, but won't your absence worry your mother and father even more?"

Allyria's stomach was too wound up for her to eat. "Please, Aunt Donella, won't you help us? They'll listen to you."

When she didn't immediately refuse, Allyria began to hope. She caught Allek's eyes as he was about to speak and shook her head for him to remain silent.

Aunt Donella wound a strand of her dark, curly hair around her finger; her eyes unfocused. "Very well," she conceded reluctantly.

Hope swelled in Allyria's chest.

Aunt Donella summoned the innkeeper and asked him for some parchment and a quill.

After scribbling a note, she called him back. "I need you to deliver a message to the palace." Now that she had made up her mind to help them, Aunt Donella gave brisk orders.

"Eat up, Allyria. I'll pack my things and we can be on our

way."

Allek crowed with delight. "You're the best, Aunt Donella. I'm glad it was you who caught us," he said before cramming another little cake in his mouth.

Aunt Donella pardoned herself and went upstairs to gather her things. Soon Allyria and Allek were seated on Seeker again, ready for adventure.

Aunt Donella insisted the inn yard in Capall was too conspicuous for portal travel. "The town is full due to the seasonal horse-trading market. We don't want word to get out that the royal children are gallivanting around the countryside."

They soon left Capall far behind. This time Allyria rode behind Aunt Donella on her horse. Allek gave Seeker his head and raced ahead, eventually turning the stallion around and walking back to them.

Allyria couldn't help but enjoy the fresh air blowing through her hair and the sunshine warming her back.

They rode most of the day, with a few breaks.

As the sun lowered in the sky, they came upon a stone marker standing sentinel at a crossroad.

Aunt Donella stopped beside it. She held out her hand wearing the mysterious trinity symbol ring on it. Mist rose from the ground at the marker's base. It swirled into a billowing circle, revealing another inn in the mist's center.

The sign creaking in the breeze read Forest Deer Inn.

Seeker trotted through the portal. Aunt Donella's mare shied but eventually followed the stallion.

After stabling the horses, they settled around a table in the inn's kitchen. A set of antlers hung on the wall with a placard below it with the words *Safe Haven* written on it.

Aunt Donella introduced the innkeeper as Evodia, a very old friend. The plump woman smelled of yeast. She had gray hair pulled back in a bun. She bustled around the kitchen and put warm bread and bowls of hot stew before them.

Allyria inhaled the savory smell of herbs and broth before digging in.

"Evodia and I go way back." Her blue eyes twinkling, Aunt Donella grinned mischievously. She told them how, at age sixteen, she had aspired to be a spy.

"A spy? You!?" Allek stared in amazement while Allyria glanced up quickly from her food.

As Aunt Donela told her story with interjections from Evodia, Allyria studied both older woman with new eyes. Of course, the Safe Haven sign meant Evodia was also a Waykeeper. They dedicated themselves to helping pilgrims and travelers, not necessarily traveling through the portals themselves, though they did that, too. How brave they must've been, risking their lives to keep Valdeor's citizens safe.

Allyria had heard many times of Aunt Donella and

Uncle Guy's brave deeds stopping an invasion from Canteor. Suddenly it felt very real now that she was on her own expedition, far from home.

"But didn't you eventually meet up with Uncle Guy on the Isle or Origin? Where we're headed? Do tell us about it." Allek leaned in, his food forgotten for the moment.

"You'll see it for yourself very soon." Aunt Donella's eyes got a faraway look. "The Isle of Origin is far beyond the seafaring routes. It's shrouded in a misty barrier. The location of it was lost for a thousand years. But Guy had a mission to find it. To restore faith in the One Who Fashioned All." At their blank looks, she smiled. "You'll understand when you get there.

"But I'll tell you something most people don't know. When pilgrims began arriving regularly to the holy fountain, I received a visit from the Guardian of Valdeor."

Allek choked on his bread.

Evodia pounded him on the back.

He sipped his drink and gasped, "You mean, the being of light that watches over all the peoples?"

Aunt Donella grinned at him. "The same. For I, too, had played a part in the turning of Canteor from a pagan land to a people of belief in the Creator."

Allyria stared at Aunt Donella. She wondered if she would have courage in the same situation. Her admiration for the fun-loving, easy-going Waykeeper grew immeasurably.

After a long day of excitement, Allyria struggled to stay awake, nodding off in the warm, cozy kitchen.

Aunt Donella sent her and Allek to bed, declaring they'd leave early the next morning for the eastern garrison, the next leg of their journey.

Drifting to sleep, Allyria was thankful Aunt Donella had come upon them and decided to guide them. Alone, Seeker couldn't take them all the way to the Isle of Origin. Unable to imagine it, Allyria wouldn't have been able to direct the stallion there. And it was probably too far for him to jump. He was only a beast, after all.

But Aunt Donella could get them to their final destination.

11 Caervale

The lush green mountains dipped into the sea. An inlet carved into the hills, allowing habitation. The whitewashed houses with red slate roofs of Caervale stretched up the towering cliffs from the harbor. The mountain tops above were invisible in the lowering clouds.

Upon disembarking the *Valiant* at Caervale, Lauryn suggested that the group should split up. She looked to Allyn, acknowledging that they were partners. He agreed.

Allyn noted that Lauryn had been overly quiet the last few weeks. She hadn't given him a chance to talk privately with her. Something was really wrong. She shared everything with him.

Xylander claimed he could glean information if he was on his own. Lauryn gave him an odd look as he trudged off. Upon their reunion at the fortress, she had defended the younger prince. Now, weeks later, she acted suspicious of him.

Everard suggested that he and Allyn buy supplies. Jarell offered to rent horses. The girls headed to the market to buy food.

Allyn turned to Everard as they headed down the small city streets. "What's with Lauryn? She seems overly cautious of Xylander. I thought he turned out to be trustworthy after all?"

"You're asking me to read Lauryn's moods?" Everard rubbed the back of his neck and gave Allyn a disbelieving look. "There have been times on this trip where she and I have attained camaraderie, only to have her withdraw angrily. I'll never understand her, even though I've known her most of her life."

"I know. But you have to look at it from her point of view. She's always seen herself as the future Reina. I think this quest has shaken Lauryn to her core. My bet is that she doesn't know who she is anymore. Or what her role will be if she loses. I know I'm struggling with that myself." Allyn gave his friend a self-deprecatory smile.

"With time and study, I'm sure either of you would make a fine ruler." Everard clapped him on the back.

Allyn narrowed his eyes at Everard. "If that's the kind of stuff you've been spouting to Lauryn, she would glower at you."

Everard looked taken aback.

"Lauryn has many good qualities that would make her a preferable ruler to me. She spends way too much time studying as it is. She needs more time for fun and friends. As do you. You two are too much alike." He counted on his fingers. "Serious. Always working for a goal. No time for relaxation. Single-minded."

Allyn shook his head. "Good thing Lauryn got over her crush on you. She needs someone to lighten her load, not scold her."

Everard's Adam's apple bobbed. "She had a crush on me? I mean, I wondered if she did when she was a teenager. She was always tagging after us." He furrowed his brow. "But you are my best friend, and she's your sister."

Allyn gazed at Everard in surprise. "So? What difference would that make?"

"You wouldn't object if I, well, made her the object of my gallantry?" Everard pulled at his collar, as if it were suddenly too tight, avoiding Allyn's eyes.

Allyn had never seen his friend act so awkward. He was always the picture of calm, manly confidence. Then again, Allyn never saw him pursue any female. Everard was masterful on the training grounds among men.

Allyn threw back his mind to Everard at social events. He often kept his eyes on Lauryn, but anyone training in the royal guards would do the same. Everard did his minimal duty by the ladies on the dance floor, then usually propped himself against the wall. Although, now Allyn thought about it, Everard always danced once with Lauryn, even if half the night passed before he could catch her without a partner.

Stopping in front of a store displaying a wide variety of various merchandise, Allyn put his hands on his hips. "If you ever show interest in a girl, I'm sure your intentions would be honorable. Not that I'd enjoy witnessing a kiss, or anything like that." He shuddered. "Are you asking my permission to pursue my sister?" He cocked his head.

Everard reddened. "Maybe. I don't know if I have a chance with her."

"Well, you have a better chance than that jackanapes, Xylander. If she wins the throne, they couldn't be married and both rule their countries with a sea between them since he's crown prince."

Allyn tapped his lips with an index finger. He couldn't help needling his friend. "Though, of course, he's a magnificent catch if she loses the throne."

"What? She'd never consider that bantam rooster." Allyn could hear Everard growl from three feet away. He had it bad for Lauryn. Only he didn't know it.

As for Lauryn, she would be lucky to have Everard at her side. For all his shyness around her, he was a good, steady, level-headed man in an emergency. Surely, she realized that by now.

Since he planted a seed in Everard's head, Allyn decided he had teased his friend enough and switched topics.

"So, back to my original question. Is Xylander trustworthy? Lauryn seems cautious around him."

Everard fingered his blade hilt. "To be honest, I don't know. But he's got us this far. And there's you and Jarell and me to watch over the girls. No matter how good a swordsman he is, it's three to one."

"Lauryn would disagree. She makes four, you know."

Everard rubbed the back of his neck. "Uh, I guess so."

Allyn smirked to see this side of Everard, floundering for the right words.

Lauryn and Giada picked their way among the market stalls. Vendors called out their wares. Chickens roamed the streets while a woman and two children tried to corral them. A donkey loaded with two baskets of cabbages brayed as the younger child dashed in front of it. The air was redolent with the smells of bread, roasting meats, dung, and salt air. Colorfully-dyed fabrics and yarns caught the eye as they swayed in the light sea breeze.

They stood before a fruit stall manned by an old woman in a colorful headscarf. When she saw Lauryn admiring it, she told Lauryn that her daughter sold the best scarves in the city and pointed out her daughter's stall across the way. Lauryn commented that they would check it out next.

Giada contemplated apples and oranges piled in a heap, indecision on her face.

"So, is there something going on between you and Xylander? I was shocked when he announced that you were engaged," Lauryn quizzed her friend.

Giada frowned. "When Xylander said it the other day, it was the first I heard of it. Father never said anything. And he'd expect Xylander to ask his permission before saying

176

anything to me. Father is old-fashioned that way!"

"I'm sure my father would be the same. They don't think of us as young ladies. We'll always be children in their eyes." Lauryn nodded sagely.

After Giada paid for the apples, they strolled to the scarf stall.

The girls sorted through the fine silk scarves, oohing and aahing over the many designs.

"But what do you think of Xylander? Do you have feelings for him?" Lauryn wanted to assess her brother's chances more than she wanted to know what Giada felt about the prince.

Xylander had seemed to waver in his resolution to marry Giada. Lauryn almost wondered if he had begun to develop feelings for her instead. But then, when reunited with Giada, he tried to dictate his cousin's actions, as if he had the right to.

The more she was in his company, the less Lauryn was likely to consider him a suitor. Even entering a long-term betrothal while they matured was distasteful to her. The prince was arrogant and self-centered. Somehow, she thought that wouldn't change with time.

Glancing at her friend, Lauryn realized she hadn't answered the question. Giada was blushing, her gaze focused distantly. Lauryn swiveled her head to see what had caught Giada's eyes. Everard and Allyn were conversing at the far end of the market square.

"Maybe you have feelings for someone else."

Giada raised her eyes to Lauryn. "You won't say anything to him, will you?" Her expression was pleading. "I don't know if he returns my feelings. I'm almost sixteen. But I doubt Father will let me have a say in who I marry." She looked depressed at the thought.

"Of course I won't betray your confidence! He may be my brother, but you are my friend. Girls keep each other's secrets."

They quickly paid for their purchases. Lauryn bought a purple scarf with gold stars sprinkled on it. Giada's was a light blue edged with white trim that complemented her eyes.

Lauryn pulled Giada into an alley when the young men began walking their way. After a few steps, the boys entered a shop, leaving the way clear again.

Pointing out a bakery, Giada donned her new headscarf and quickly crossed the road and entered. Lauryn, draping her hair with the purple scarf, was a step behind her.

"What about you?" Giada tilted her head at Lauryn as they stood in line. "You spent the trip with Xylander. A marriage with him would benefit both Valdeor and Canteor, I suppose. Although I would hate leaving my country for a foreign land unless it were a true love match."

"Every once in a while, I find myself warming up to him. But, to be honest, he rubs me the wrong way." Lauryn crossed her arms. "I simply don't trust him."

"And your other traveling companion? Sparks of a different kind seem to ignite whenever you argue." Giada's lips turned up in a sly manner as she looked sideways at her friend.

"Everard and I have known each other forever." Lauryn concentrated on counting out buns and putting them on the counter.

"So have Allyn and I." Giada's voice dropped. "Yet somehow it's different when we're together now."

"I saw how my twin looked at you when you first appeared in Samarantha. The little shy girl with braids was suddenly a poised young lady. He couldn't wait to sit beside you." Lauryn bumped her shoulder into the other girl's.

"And Everard follows you with his eyes when he thinks you aren't looking," Giada shot back.

"Does he?" Lauryn smiled secretly.

The store bell jangled.

A voice behind her made Lauryn jump. "There you are. We've finished our shopping."

Turning quickly, Lauryn overbalanced the bag of bread. Before it could spill to the floor, Everard grabbed it, their hands overlapping. She froze as a flush crept across her cheeks.

"That's a pretty scarf." Allyn reached for Giada's satchel. "Here, let me take that." He grinned. "What else do we need to buy? I saw a cheesemonger next door. Shall we?" He led the way, Giada following obediently in his wake, a look of devotion on her face.

Lauryn schooled her face into a bland expression. At least she hoped that's what she projected as Everard disentangled her bag from her arm, looping it over his shoulder.

"Ladies first." He held open the door, and she dropped her eyes before his.

Not knowing his feelings left her at a disadvantage. Most of the time he acted like an older brother, scolding and bossing her around. But he had jumped, too, when they touched. He was suddenly acting awkward around her. It could mean he was equally attracted to her, or it could mean nothing.

She had years of practice at suppressing her yearning. She called on it now.

Besides, as the quest was nearing the end, she needed to focus on what was important. She was born to be Reina. She had spent her life preparing for the role. She would do what was right for Valdeor. Including who she married. Emotions only got in the way.

Early the next morning, Lauryn woke up before the sun. Restless, she quickly dressed, leaving Giada asleep in the next bed. She snuck down the inn's narrow stairway, and into the courtyard for fresh air.

Anticipation made her limbs tingle as they neared their

journey's end. Now on Canteor soil, the mountains loomed overhead. Somewhere up there lived the elusive firebird!

"Impressive, aren't they?" a male voice said behind her.

Lauryn turned to see Xylander staring at the snowy peaks.

He glanced at her. "How committed are you to winning this quest?"

She startled at his question. Her life's purpose had always been to step into her mother's shoes. She had devoted her time to learning statecraft, etiquette, history, and diplomacy.

If she were honest with herself, she had enjoyed the freedom this quest brought her. Other than the pirates imprisoning her, she had no pressure from the court or anyone else to be anything but herself. No measuring every word, keeping her emotions under wraps, living up to other's expectations. No schedules, no lessons.

Yet, if she wasn't chosen Reina, what would she do with her life? She couldn't roam the kingdoms seeking adventure.

Homesickness washed over her. Was Mother better? Worse? How did Father cope? Did Lysa miss their time together? Did Allyria look after their youngest sister in her absence?

"I'm ready for this mission to be over," Lauryn admitted.

"Are you ready to steal a march on your brother?" Xylander raised an eyebrow. "If so, I will escort you to the firebird. We can leave before the others awake."

Lauryn stiffened. *Desert the others?*

But how else was she to win? She bit her lip, undecided. It seemed like a betrayal somehow.

Leave and win. Or stay and forfeit her right to the throne.

"I'll get my things and meet you at the stable." Lauryn swallowed her guilt as she crept back upstairs. *This was a race! The best person wins. She* must *be that person.*

Careful not to wake Giada, Lauryn dragged her satchel from under her bed. Walking to the stable, Lauryn found Xylander packed and ready to go.

Once mounted, Xylander led them through the streets that led toward the foothills. At the end of town, the path diverged left and right. Xylander took the right path.

The trail gradually grew steeper. When the sun arose, it sparkled on the sea below them. Somewhere across that vast expanse was home and her loved ones.

Rounding a bend, they came upon a small village nestled in the hills.

"I learned yesterday that I can hire guides here to take us the rest of the way." Xylander drew his horse up before the largest house and dismounted.

Lauryn searched through her pack for something to eat. She forced herself to chew a chunk of dried bread, even though she didn't have an appetite.

She should have left a note. The others might worry about her.

Was Xylander trustworthy? At first, she thought not. Then she changed her mind as he fought beside her. But lately he hadn't been cooperative. He had become the arrogant prince of their early days. Now, he was willing to help her. Why the sudden change? What was in it for him?

Lauryn shoved those thoughts aside. Her parents had given her a quest. Bring back a firebird's feather. The first one who did so would be ruler. No sharing the spoils.

Allyn was perfectly capable of completing the quest. With Giada's help, he had as much of a chance as Lauryn did.

Stiffening her spine, she stared at the door Xylander had disappeared into.

In a short while it opened. The prince came toward her, two men at his heels. The first man, with silver-streaked black hair, was older than Father by at least a decade. He had a look of command about him. Trailing behind the other two, a burly man deferred to them.

Xylander spoke in low tones with the leader as they approached. The prince frowned, an expression of indecision on his face. The older man broke off their conversation to stare at Lauryn with intensely dark eyes. Something in his demeanor changed and he shared a look with Xylander.

"I will take you myself to the place. It will be an honor." His grin became smug. He sent a covert glance back at Lauryn before he reentered the house.

A chill went down her spine, not from the cold morning breeze. She didn't trust their guide.

Under her breath, she said so to Xylander when he mounted his horse.

"Nonsense. He's the most experienced guide in the village. We can't waste time looking for someone more cheerful to allay your suspicions." His voice was dismissive, though Xylander didn't look her in the eye as he spoke. "Your brother likely isn't far behind us. We must keep moving."

Her gut squirmed with foreboding. Yet the thought of Allyn already following their trail tamped down her lingering fear. He, Everard, and Jarell would eventually catch up with her group.

Lauryn probably had an hour or less head start. They'd already agreed to leave at dawn, which had passed some time ago.

Within minutes, they departed the village, the guide in the lead. Fifteen minutes later, hearing hoof beats, Lauryn turned around expecting to see her twin riding toward them. Instead, a rock settled in her stomach as another twelve men on horseback joined their group. Some had swords strapped on their backs. Others carried clubs.

Apprehension dug claws into her chest. She guided her mount to ride closer to Xylander. "Who are those men?" She kept her voice low.

He held himself stiffly in the saddle but answered casually, "Joad, our guide, said the mountain pass is home to bandits. It's safer to travel with armed guards. We're not the only ones who have sought the firebird over the years.

Bandits prey on the unwary."

"Do you trust these people?" She wanted to gauge his reaction.

"My advice to you is do not trust *anyone*." His eyes glinted with a warning before he glanced away. "I won't let anything happen to you." He suppressed some emotion. "Follow my lead, Lauryn. I am doing what's best for everyone." But she thought she discerned guilt in his eyes.

He was holding something back from her.

She suddenly wished she had asked Ever to accompany her instead of leaving with Xylander.

Joad, in the lead, glanced back at them. Xylander's expression changed into a tight smile. Something seemed insincere in his face. He maneuvered his horse to ride beside the guide.

But Lauryn could see the bunched muscles in Xylander's back. He didn't fully trust Joad either. Xylander played some game that Lauryn didn't understand. Her trust in him wavered. But she had committed to this course of action. She could do nothing at this point but play along.

Keeping her gaze straight ahead, she wore her court mask of indifference. She regretted not alerting Ever, at least, to her plans. Of course, he would've tried to stop her. If only she could contact him.

An idea formed in her mind. She would leave breadcrumbs on their trail.

12 Portal to the Isles

Allyria and Allek dug into a hearty breakfast of fresh-baked scones, eggs, and bacon, which the grandmotherly Evodia made for them. The cozy kitchen had a teapot on the boil over a cheerful fire, jars of preserves on shelves, herbs hanging from the ceiling, and a cupboard displaying plates.

It was truly a Safe Haven, as the sign declared.

Evodia pushed the jampot at Allyria. The mulberry jam tasted as if it were fresh off the vine.

"So, what's the plan?" Allek scooped a large spoonful of jam onto his scone.

"The eastern garrison, along the coast, is our destination this morning." Aunt Donella sipped her tea. "We should leave soon. We have several stops to make."

After breakfast, Evodia hugged them all and gave them food wrapped in oiled skin to keep it dry.

Having retrieved their packs, the twins followed Aunt Donella to the stable. Allek helped saddle the stallion and the mare. Aunt Donella gave each one a sugar cube and rubbed their noses. She hoisted Allyria behind Allek on Seeker, then mounted her own horse.

She walked the horses to a stone marker. Aunt Donella activated the portal. The mist pooled and opened a vista of a stone fortress on a seaside cliff.

The horses stepped through into the tunnel's blackness. Allyria's head spun, disoriented. She grasped Allek's waist and squeezed her eyes shut. Suddenly, a cool breeze wafted around her and she smelled the sea's distinct scent. A seagull screamed overhead.

She opened her eyes. They were on a hard-packed dirt trail which led over a hill and down again to the fortress gate.

Aunt Donella guided her horse south, perpendicular from the garrison. "We'll travel down to Laketown. It's safer to take a ship to the islands rather than jump such distances. That's what Uncle Guy and I found out over time. Too many jumps in a row, or too long a trip through the portals, is hard on the body."

"Oh, I thought we'd be there tonight." Allek muttered.

"Technically, we could. But you'd need several days to recover. Or we can spend the same amount of time sailing there." Aunt Donella pushed her curly, dark hair back from the stiff sea breeze as she rode alongside them.

Allyria nudged her brother. "You've always wanted to sail the ocean."

He turned his head and grinned back at her. "I still do. I guess this is my chance to do it."

They rode all day. The first leg of the journey was parallel to the sea. Allyria had read about it, but the enormity took her breath away. The sun sparkled on the endless stretch of water. The rhythmic sound of the waves soothed her worry. She hoped Mother wasn't too anxious on their account.

After breaking for a delicious lunch of a cold meat-filled pastry which Evodia had packed, they remounted. The road turned away from the sea and went inland. Soon they were on a wooded path which eventually led to a mountain lake.

They stopped on its banks for the night. Allek was excited to camp outdoors. He gathered a great many sticks and showed off his skill in lighting a fire.

"Are there w-wolves?" Allyria couldn't control the tremble in her voice as she glanced around in the twilight. Adventures in books had always sounded fun. But now? She had never realized how comfortable her bed was when she was faced with sleeping on the ground. Even if Allek had piled up pine boughs for her to lie on.

"They don't come down this time of year to the foothills where we are on Lake Genesay. They are found higher in the Blue Range Mountains." Aunt Donella assured her.

The mountains rose in a purplish-blue haze across the entire horizon to the west.

For dinner, they ate sliced lamb on crunchy rolls. Evodia had even included a flask containing milk for the children.

They settled down for the night. Allyria tossed and

turned, anxiety spiking at every noise. Seeker snuffled a few yards away. Surely the intelligent stallion would alert them to danger. With that reassuring thought, she finally drifted to sleep.

The next morning, they rode partly around the lake until Aunt Donella led them to a ferry station. She paid the grizzled old man. They and the horses were soon aboard a flat-bottomed boat floating across the lake. Lake Genesay's size amazed Allyria. Obviously, it wasn't as large as the ocean, but crossing it took them three hours.

Mounting again, they followed a rutted path to the east.

Thunder rumbled, although the sun shone. The sound grew louder as they approached a cliff's edge. Then Allyria understood where the sound originated. It wasn't a thunderstorm after all. A stream fed from the lake poured over the cliff for two hundred feet. A rainbow glistened in the spray. The roar was deafening here.

A city crouched at the base of the cliff.

The height made Allyria dizzy. How were they ever to get down there?

Since shouting directions was useless, Aunt Donella pointed, and led them to a steep path.

Allyria feared she would be sick. The narrow track, with its hairpin turns down the cliff face, looked impossible to traverse.

"Close your eyes, Allyria. Just breathe. Seeker is sure-footed." Allek must've felt her arms clench around his middle. Or he felt her anxiety through their twin bond.

She hung onto her brother, her eyes squeezed shut, and prayed to the One Who Fashioned All that they wouldn't slip and fall hundreds of feet to lie broken on the rocks. She focused on the sun's warmth on her back and Seeker's steady, plodding gait.

Even with her eyes shut, she knew when the path veered close to the falls. The cool water sprayed her skin. And the sound and spray retreated when the path turned away. Halfway down, when they neared the waterfall, she opened her eyes.

Across from them a white mountain goat calmly chewed its cud. At its feet on the ledge grew little bluebells. Calm washed over Allyria as she looked out over the ocean as they turned in that direction. She saw a ship's majestic sails headed toward the harbor. She kept her eyes open after that, trusting the stallion, and soaked in the marvelous view.

Laketown houses nestled in the hills which eventually ended at the cliffs and spectacular waterfall. The inhabitants had painted their quarried stone houses with bright colors.

Along a sweeping crescent of beach and rock, the city overlooked the sea. Wharves extended into the water. Many ships rode at anchor in the busy seaport.

Allyria stood at the rail of a ship.

She was sad to leave Seeker behind, but Aunt Donella

said Laketown's waykeeper would return him to the palace stables.

Allyria watched Laketown and the coast slip beyond the horizon. She had sailed on a ship down a river with Father, but she had never been out to sea. She walked along the bulkhead, crossed her arms on the edge, and watched the prow cut through the water, throwing up spray.

She wondered where her siblings were. Were they crossing the sea this very moment like her?

Allek took to the ship like a duck to water. Shading her eyes, she looked at the mast top where he perched in the crow's nest.

That evening, he was excited about sleeping in a hammock with the sailors in the hold. Allyria was more comfortable sharing a cabin with Aunt Donella.

Allyria hardly saw Allek the rest of the week. He worked alongside the sailors at any job they gave him. Allyria whiled away the hours playing a strategic board game with Aunt Donella, when she wasn't outside watching for dolphins. Sitting under the canopy of stars at night, Aunt Donella told her stories of her life before meeting Uncle Guy, and her days as a slave.

On the seventh day, the watchman sighted land. Soon, a string of islands appeared on the port side. They sailed another day until they reached Cressava, the biggest isle.

A white castle perched above a town with a harbor deep enough for their ship to dock. Allyria's gaze was drawn to a volcano rising in the distance like a monstrous beast ready to pounce on the dwellings below. Lush green jungle crept up the sleeping giant, whose top was wreathed in a cloud.

Disembarking, they made their way into town. The two-storied wooden buildings seemed to be leaning inward from opposite sides of the narrow street. The streets didn't follow any pattern, all higgledy-piggledy, cobbled together.

Allyria thought it very foreign compared to Mintala with its grid layout. She could easily get lost here.

Aunt Donella led them away from the rough area along the harbor to an inn closer to the castle.

Entering the taproom, Allyria heard her brother's stomach grumble as he walked beside her, and she salivated at the tempting aromas.

Dark-skinned islanders in family groups sat together around tables, while single, white sailors clustered around the bar.

Their serving girl wore a bright, yellow wrap that came to her knees. She had a red flower tucked behind her ear in her dark braids. Her teeth gleamed white in her cinnamon face when she gave them a friendly grin and asked for their order.

The three soon dug heartily into seafood chowder and buttered hot rolls. The native girl poured them glasses of purple liquid from a pitcher. Allyria was pleasantly surprised at the tangy juice.

Seeing her expression, the island girl asked, "Have you

never tasted dragon blood fruit? We grow it on the islands."

"It's delicious." Allyria smiled back at her.

Since it was early when they finished dinner, Aunt Donella took them on a tour of the town. It was bigger than Allyria had realized.

Allek suggested they purchase a large flask to carry the healing water. "Surely the more we have, the better it will work." They entered the market square. It took them a while to find a stall that sold what they wanted. Allek carried the simple amphora from a pottery shop.

"You simply must visit the castle before you leave." Aunt Donella strolled uphill toward the castle overlooking the town. Seashells of all sizes and varieties were plastered into the walls. Even the entrance was in the shape of a scalloped shell.

"From the gardens the view is spectacular." She led them around the side to an ornamental gate entwined with dolphins and mermaids playing in stylized waves. Their feet crunched on the path made of tiny shells. Bushes heavy with exotic smelling blooms were interspersed with statues of nymphs on pedestals. The outer wall separated them from a cliff dropping off to the harbor below. The wall was studded with seashells.

The town was spread out in a half-circle around the turquoise harbor. Looking over her shoulder, Allyria shivered at the volcano looming above them. The jungle's humidity pressed down like a blanket. Strange bird calls heightened the feeling of foreignness.

Instead of returning the way they had come, Aunt Donella opened a gate that led to steep steps cut into the cliff. They descended and ended in a cove.

Walking along the shore as the sun lowered, Allyria couldn't help smiling. She had read of such places, but could hardly believe she was actually here. If only Mother were well and her illness didn't weigh on Allyria's soul, she would enjoy it more.

They eventually made it back to the inn. Allyria thought she'd sleep peacefully and deeply back on land but she dreamed she heard a female voice calling out to her, *"Help me! Someone help me!"*

There was a wealth of grief and fear in the cry. Someone close to Allyria was suffering. In her dream, she couldn't make out whom, but the voice was familiar. Mother?

Allyria ran through the forest, the tree limbs scraping her, holding her back from running. Her legs dragged, never going fast enough. Reaching out her arms, she pulled herself along, grabbing branches. And always somewhere ahead was the pleading for succor.

I'm coming! Hold on.

She woke with a start as a hand shook her. "Allyria, wake up."

She groaned and opened her eyes. Sunshine streamed into the room from the open curtains. Aunt Donella's face leaned over her, etched with a frown.

"You were moaning in your sleep. Bad dream?" Aunt Donella walked across the room and washed her hands in the basin provided for ablutions.

"Yes. I have a feeling time is running out for Mother."

"Don't worry. Trust in the One Who Fashioned All. We'll head to the Isle of Origin after breaking our fast."

On a quiet street in Cressava, the three travelers stepped through the mist into a humid, noisy jungle. A brightly-colored macaw squawked and flew away in a flutter of turquoise and yellow feathers. Other birds grew silent at their appearance, but within moments the cacophony started up again.

The trees were strangely-shaped, with tops like a parasol. When Allek asked about them, Aunt Donella explained the natives called them dragon's blood trees, same as the juice they had enjoyed yesterday.

Aunt Donella confidently strode along the overgrown path that led from the portal deeper into the brush.

After walking for a short time, tiny midges swarmed, drawn to their sweat, as the damp heat surrounded them like a steam bath.

Drawings in Allyria's books didn't do justice to the real-life jungle. Exotic fragrances tickled her nose. It smelled like all the palace courtiers' perfumes mingled together in one place. The leaves of the trees and bushes were of every shade of green, from emerald to jade. Flowers added splashes of color, as did the bright, rainbow of feathered birds.

Forty-five minutes later, the jungle came to a sudden end. They stood on a canyon's edge. A narrow path led steeply down to a bridge which spanned the river below, a waterfall churning under it.

On the canyon's other side, a magnificent building seemed to shimmer in the light. The front was round with a dome, pierced with colored-glass windows, and topped with a twisting spiral. Three stained-glass windows were on each side of the enormous wooden door. Above it was the tri-fold symbol in red, yellow, and blue. The shrine's back end was in the shape of a rectangle. At each corner were four twisted, white spirals. More colorful, stained-glass windows studded the structure's brilliant white walls and penetrated even the roof, giving it a pop of color.

"The legendary, hidden shrine! It's more lovely than I imagined!" Allyria had heard tales of how Uncle Guy found it when it had been lost for centuries.

"Seeing it after an absence, it never grows old. I have traveled all over Valdeor and Canteor, and there is nothing comparable to it." Aunt Donella smiled.

Allyria glanced around to see Allek's reaction. It was unlike him to be quiet. Then she realized he wasn't there. She scanned the area, then gazed up.

There, thirty feet back on the trail, Allek had climbed partway up a dragon's blood tree. A small monkey chattered at her brother from several branches above him.

Aunt Donella followed her gaze. "Allek!"

"Don't worry, Aunt. Allek climbs like a monkey himself. Mother and Father gave up forbidding him a long time ago." Allyria tried to allay Aunt Donella's fear.

"My son was the same when he was younger. But, it's not only the height." Aunt Donella lifted her skirts and ran toward Allek. "Watch out Allek! Those monkeys bite!"

But her warning was too late. Allek had already reached for the little monkey, who stopped scolding him and promptly bit Allek's hand as he touched its leg.

Undeterred, Allek held out a bread chunk in his other hand. The monkey snatched it and ran higher up the tree. It spun the bread around a few times, as if studying a foreign substance, then settled down to eat the treat.

"Come down, Allek!"

Reluctantly, her brother obeyed Aunt Donella. "I would've made friends with it. Eventually." He scowled, then his expression morphed into a resigned look.

Allyria rolled her eyes. "We didn't come all this way for you to find a new pet. Mother is depending on us."

Allek dropped down beside them. "How can she depend on us when she doesn't know what we're doing? She didn't ask us to go on this quest."

Allyria huffed. Allek could be so literal.

As they walked to the shrine, Allyria described her dream from last night. "I think Mother called me."

"It's only a nightmare. Not a vision. In fact, are you sure it was Mother?" Allek started first down the cliff path, offering his hand to Allyria over the rough spots.

"Nooo," she drew out the vowel sound. "But who else could it be?"

"I dunno. You're worried about nothing, Allyria. A dream." Allek dismissed her concerns with a wave of his hand.

But her worry was like an itch under her skin. Mother needed a cure. Now.

13 Mount Merione

*S*o Lauryn never said anything to you about leaving? Not even a hint?" Alloryn gazed into Giada's blue eyes. They brimmed with anxiety. But she was telling the truth.

Allyn only asked her for the third time because he couldn't believe Lauryn would disappear without a word. *At least, not willingly.*

The two of them stood at the foot of the stairs, the inn's eating hall on their right and the door to the stableyard on the left.

"No. I awoke, and she was gone. Her pack is missing, too." Giada clutched her hands together. "Do you think she's in trouble?"

Everard entered through the door leading to the stableyard, scowling as he heard Giada's remark.

Jarell tromped down the stairs. "No sign of his High and Mighty prince. His room is cleared out." He scratched his nose. "I don't know why Lauryn would go off with him, but it looks as if she did."

Everard crossed his arms. "Two horses are gone as

well."

"I couldn't help but overhear you." A freckled boy of twelve appeared at Allyn's elbow. "I'm the stable master's son. I saddled up two horses this morn for a lovely woman and a young man."

Everard growled.

When the boy didn't continue speaking, Allyn withdrew a gold coin from his pouch. "Did you hear anything they said? Accidently, of course."

The boy's eyes didn't stray from the coin. He licked his lips. "Well, I couldn't help hearing the young man say they could find guides in Pineridge." A shiver passed over him. "'Tis a dangerous place. Those in the mountains still worship the old god. You couldn't get me to step foot in those hills. They say the old god himself lives there. His power flames up and you can see his fire from here."

"And how do we get to Pineridge?" It dawned on Allyn that Lauryn had stolen a march on him.

The boy gave them directions, and Allyn flipped the coin into his waiting hands. The boy scampered away.

"It seems Lauryn means to win this hunt." Allyn grimaced, but he understood her desire to be crown princess. "Is everybody ready to set out? At least we know where to find a guide."

Jarell shook his head. "So Lauryn didn't want you along. Why would she take Xylander with her instead of me or Everard?"

Giada gave him a look of disbelief. "Obviously, Xylander knows where the firebird is." Her expression fell. "I wish she had asked me instead of my cousin. He wants something out of this; you can be sure. He doesn't do anything out of the goodness of his heart."

As they picked up their gear, Allyn heard Everard say under his breath, "I wish she would've trusted me."

The sun had risen while they were mounting up. Allyn had his foot in the stirrup when Jarell gasped and grabbed Everard's bridle.

"What—?"

"Your girth strap has been cut!" Jarell wore an expression of shocked disbelief.

Everard dismounted and inspected it for himself. He straightened, his brow thunderous. "It looks as if it were tampered with."

Jarell inspected the next horse. "Giada, the ring on your bridle is snapped. Any stress on it and it will break loose!" Jarell met Allyn's eyes over her horse's head.

Allyn and Jarell inspected their saddles and found the same signs of mischief. Meanwhile, Everard brought over the stable master and showed him the damage.

The man paled. He disclaimed any blame. It took a while for them to find replacements. All the saddles in the stable belonged to the patrons. The stable master sent his son to awaken the town's saddlemaker so they could buy new ones.

Nearly two mores hour were lost. Anger built inside Allyn at the trick Xylander had played on them. It had to be him. Allyn had never trusted the Canteor prince, and this substantiated it.

When they finally rode the trail toward Pineridge, Allyn maneuvered his horse beside Everard. "You traveled with Xylander. What could be his motivation for helping Lauryn win? Other than the fact that he doesn't like me." Allyn's gaze strayed to Giada, riding behind them. Xylander was jealous of Allyn's closeness to the young princess. Especially since he seemed set on marrying her. Yet why hadn't he asked Giada to join them? She was Allyn's only hope of finding the firebird's whereabouts.

Everard scowled. Allyn could tell he was concentrating, so he remained quiet.

"Lauryn told me he said something about a firebird feather when they met Irdek. The rulers of his country wear it in their turban. It supposedly has magical abilities, according to the Canteoran legends."

"So, Xylander does have a motive." Allyn rubbed the back of his neck. "He wants a feather for himself. He's the crown prince and heir to the throne, but maybe the feather gives him more credibility. The same as Lauryn or I."

"Xylander seems touchy about his father's past. Any mention of being a slave sets the prince off," Everard said.

"I've heard rumors at court that there's a growing Canteor faction demanding a pureblood heir to the throne."

Allyn put the pieces together. "If so, Xylander faces opposition because his father was disinherited by the King of Samarantha. A magical feather might boost his claim of suitability."

The Canteor prince's presence on their quest made more sense. Allyn assumed Aunt Donella wanted Xylander to join them for her own reasons. Perhaps she suspected that Xylander knew where the firebird lived. But now Allyn considered that Xylander might've wheedled Aunt Donella into including him. Joining a group expedition had greater possibility for success than hunting for it on his own.

But why hadn't Xylander been open about it? It isn't like the firebird had only one feather.

Allyn had a foreboding feeling that there was more to the story than he knew. And it had something to do with Lauryn. Or why hadn't Xylander snuck off on his own?

He was even more sure of it when they arrived in the village of Pineridge. None of the villagers would open their doors. He caught sight of faces peeking from curtains. If he turned his head that way, the fabric dropped back in place.

One oily man seemed anxious that they hire him. But his sly eyes slipped away from direct contact.

"Quite the friendly town," Jarell commented.

"We'll find our own way," Allyn said. When they passed through the village, he told Jarell and Everard, "Use your scouting skills. If Lauryn's suspicions were aroused as mine were, she'll try to leave us a trail to follow."

An hour further down the trail, they entered the valley hemmed in by mountain ranges. The trail split three ways. One right, one left, and one forward.

Allyn turned to Giada as she stared into the distance. "Which way?"

Giada pointed at one of the peaks above them. "That's the firebird's home. I saw that mountain top in the mirror pool's vision." Giada wore a look of vindication as she glanced at Jarell. "See, it's canted to the left."

The peak did have a distinct look. The jagged granite tip rose above the mountain sides covered in snow.

"You were right, and I was wrong. Without your help, we wouldn't have found our way here." Jarell nodded at her reluctantly. He didn't like to apologize or admit when he was mistaken. Allyn realized he had matured on this journey.

There were signs on the trail of many horses recently traveling this way.

A few hours later, Allyn was ready to call a break.

Jarell halted his horse. "Look!" he pointed ahead at the trail winding up the mountain.

A line of mounted riders rode single file up an incline. Allyn couldn't distinguish Lauryn at this distance, though he knew it must be her group. His gut roiled at her unwanted entourage.

"I count sixteen riders." Everard growled. "Fourteen so-called guides are with them. More like guards to keep Lauryn from escaping." He clenched his hands on his reins. "I estimate they have a two-hour head start on us."

Another half an hour's hard ride on the flat plain brought them to a crossroads. The hard-packed road didn't show hoof prints.

But as much as he wanted to find his twin, Allyn knew that a dangerous situation lay before them. Probably the worst they faced on this quest.

Why would Xylander gather a large group of men at this point? Had he contacted them beforehand? What was the young prince's role in all this?

Frustration built in Allyn's gut until a glint of something bright caught his eye. Intuition told him Lauryn left him a clue.

Although he'd made it his responsibility to look after Giada on this trip, she was better off far from a fight. He wanted both Jarell and Everard at his side when they faced Xylander's men. But he had to protect Giada.

"We'd better split up. Jarell, you and Giada go left. Ever and I will take the path to the right." He swallowed. His brother was more than capable of taking care of his girlfriend. He admitted what she meant to him, at least to himself. Why deny it any longer?

He could hear Lauryn's voice in his head. *Hurry, Allyn. Help! Beware!*

He and Everard started up the path. He pulled his

mount up short, dismounted, and retrieved the glittering object. Gold glittered in his hand. *Lauryn's hairpin!*

"I'll call the others." Everard swung his horse's head around but Allyn grabbed his bridle. Everard's expression clouded over with concern.

"No. Giada is best away from this. But she wouldn't stay behind if I asked." Allyn remounted, placing the hairpin in his pocket.

Everard's brow cleared. "Thanks for picking Jarell over me to babysit her. Although with your feelings for her, I'm surprised you didn't ask me to guard her. I do wield a better sword." He quirked an eyebrow.

"Jarell can handle any trouble, especially since I sent them on the wrong path." Allyn chuckled.

"So, we only split up to keep Giada safe?" Everard sounded amused.

"Lauryn's danger is greater than Giada's. She might need your sword to save her."

Everard sobered.

After riding in silence for a while, Ever grunted. "This path you chose. It was a twin thing, wasn't it?"

Allyn sent him a lopsided grin. "No. I saw her hairpin twinkling on the ground and figured that Lauryn left us a message." He pulled it out and showed Everard. "There is a chance I could be wrong. But how many mountain girls wear golden pins?"

"She must be desperate. That's the hairpin with the

hidden blade." A strong emotion passed over Everard's face. "Your sister is very resilient. Her daring takes my breath away." He recounted how she walked on a narrow ledge from her prison cell to his, during the storm.

"Yeah. Sometimes I don't know whether to hug her or shake her."

Everard snorted.

The thought of his sister's creative bravado lightened Allyn's heart somewhat. Lauryn would use anything she could to her advantage, knowing that her brothers and friends wouldn't give up on her.

We're coming, Lauryn. Hold on!

Allyn wouldn't let his sister down.

14 Firebird

*T*he air grew thinner as they mounted higher. Lauryn raised the hood of her warm cloak to combat the chill. The valley below seemed small from this distance. As she guided her horse on a hairpin turn on the narrow path, she thought she caught a glimpse of riders far below. *It had to be her brothers! Everard! They'd followed.*

The knot in her stomach loosened.

But she didn't let her guard down. Not after the snatches of conversation she had heard between Xylander and Joad during the many hours of riding.

The men with them weren't guides. Not in the strict sense. Though they did know the way to the firebird's nest.

No, they were worshipers, followers of the old god, Panmin.

Canteor had been a pagan country until the year Lauryn was born. Aunt Donella and Prince Gensard had saved the crown princess, giving her the water of regeneration while she lay dying, stabbed by a slave. The healing of Princess Sefira, by the water from the shrine of the One Who Fashioned All, convinced the nation that Panmin was a hollow myth—a golden statue with no power over life and death. Unlike the true God who brought Sefira back to perfect health.

But pockets of Panmin followers had gone underground. Rumors of squashed rebellions had reached the court of Valdeor over the years. Xylander's great uncle had been executed for fomenting a rebellion. He had wanted to gain the crown for himself, claiming he was the last pureblood royal.

Lauryn feared that these pagans had decided that Xylander was the perfect candidate to lead the rebellion. Although why he would need to when he was already the crown prince baffled her.

He had spoken of his father's slavery. She recalled his insistence that his father Leander was born a prince. Was Xylander trying to prove he was a pureblood? Or was his vanity and youth making him a pawn in Joad's deadly game?

Lauryn's thoughts were interrupted as they reached the end of the trail. A wide mountain ledge spread before them, the size of a stadium, strewn with boulders and clumps of grass. The pinnacle of the mountain jutted up from a granite cliff at the far side of the space.

The group dismounted. Some men assembled a tent, while others built a pyre of branches.

Lauryn's eyes were drawn to a giant nest which sat halfway up the peak. A purple lump was all she saw of the legendary firebird, if that was what it truly was.

She stood rooted to the spot, emotions swirling through her as she faced the end of the journey. A sense of awe filled her. The firebird really existed, and she had found it first.

"Magnificent, isn't it?" Xylander came to stand beside her. Longing filled his expression as he stared at the nest.

Pulling his gaze away, he turned to her. "This is a momentous day. Let us prepare."

Lauryn followed Xylander to the newly erected tent. A slender rider dismounted and approached them. Raising up from a deep bow, a young woman faced Lauryn.

"My name is Inka. I am here to serve you. Come, I will prepare food for you." She opened the flap and motioned Lauryn to enter. Xylander followed her in.

Someone had covered the ground with cushions and rugs. Lauryn sat down on one, cross-legged.

Inka lowered the flap, shutting them inside the tent. She removed the waterskin from her shoulder and offered it to Lauryn. Thirsty after the long ride, Lauryn took a big swallow. She choked when she realized it was wine. Not offered anything else to drink, she took a cautious sip.

Xylander chose a cushion beside Lauryn and lowered himself onto it.

He took her hand and gazed intently into her eyes. "You like me, don't you, Lauryn?"

She blinked at the strange question. He was handsome. His brown eyes stared into hers. His dark eyebrows winged up, contrasted against his bronze skin. He was definitely attractive, but she didn't entirely trust him.

He seemed satisfied even when she didn't answer, reading her expression as approval.

"When we arrived at the village, the inhabitants recognized me. They declared that if I were a pureblood, I need to follow the religion of my ancestors. If I did, they would be loyal to me. If I followed the old ways, their god would make me king. With their backing, I can create an empire greater than Canteor has ever seen." The light of ambition shone in his eyes.

"But I want you at my side. As my empress." He kissed the knuckles of the hand he still held. "Say you'll marry me and we can rule both our kingdoms jointly. Your glory and renown will be greater than even your mother's."

Lauryn felt a moment of dizziness as she took in what he was saying. Marry Xylander? Give up her family and her home? Everything in her rebelled.

"I'm sorry, Xylander. I cannot marry you." She tried to say it kindly but firmly. He gave her a look of disappointment, dropping her hand. She shuddered as he flushed with anger. She had never seen him look this way at her before, with such disdain.

Joad came in and joined them. Behind him, Inka carried in a tray of food.

Inka offered Lauryn more wine in a bowl, and she sipped it, hoping it would give her courage for whatever came next.

The men entered into a discussion about the firebird and the best way to approach it.

Feeling detached, the worry and tension Lauryn had struggled with on their way here dissipated.

Her stomach growled. She didn't remember why she hadn't touched the food. She reached out and took a hunk of bread and dipped it in a gooey sauce. The spicy flavor exploded in her mouth. She licked her fingers.

Xylander gave her a strange look. Lauryn smirked back at him. What if she didn't show perfect manners? They weren't in a palace. They ate in a tent in a remote part of the world.

The burdens of her royal upbringing seemed too heavy to bear. Couldn't she ever be Lauryn the unknown? She hummed under her breath as the girl, Inka, held out the wine bowl again. Lauryn slurped from it and giggled at the sound.

Joad's voice seemed to come from a distance. "The drug is beginning to work. She will become complacent to every command." He leaned forward and his face was out of focus, the nose stretching to enormous size. She giggled again.

The prince's frown seemed all out of proportion. "Will there be lasting effects?"

They seemed awfully serious about some girl's future. Lauryn wondered idly why she wasn't more concerned.

The men finished eating and stood to go. Joad looked like a toad with his bulging eyes and wide smile from ear to ear. "Prepare her for the ceremony."

Lauryn put her hands on her hips as she sat at his feet. "No. I'm shick and tired of c-ceremonies." She yawned. "You may go." She sweepingly waved her hand at them to depart. She was a princess. She outranked them.

Xylander had a quiet but intense conversation with Joad, who shook his head. After a few moments, Joad seemed to win the argument. Lauryn couldn't interpret the look Xylander gave her over his shoulder as he walked away. *Regret? Guilt? Worry? Resentment? A combination of them all?*

Inka helped Lauryn out of her clothes and changed them for a long white gown that covered Lauryn from her neck to her ankles. Inka then wrapped a silver cord around her waist.

The girl made Lauryn sit while she undid her braid, brushing her hair with long strokes.

Lauryn relaxed at the feel of the brushstrokes. Mother used to do the same when she was a little girl.

Mother. She needed something from Lauryn. Something important. She wished she could remember what.

As Inka poured aromatic nard into her scalp and massaged it in, Lauryn released her worries and let her thoughts float free.

At the back of her mind, a thought niggled, but she couldn't grasp it. The effort was too much work.

Lauryn had lost track of time. The last thing she remembered was the girl brushing her hair. Now the girl whose name she had forgotten, if she ever knew it, led her across the flat area to the peak's base. Six men with scimitars accompanied them.

The men gathered in a semicircle around a long, rectangular stone perched on boulders on its four corners. How strange to find a table here in the wilderness.

Nearby was a pen with a single goat inside. He let out a bleat.

Lauryn noted the change in the men. They had garbed themselves in long, black garments that sucked all the light from the air. Ceremonial robes. They had donned black turbans glinting with silver moon pins.

The girl had her stop beside the stone slab. The weathered granite had four iron loops—two in the middle and two at one end. Lauryn should understand its significance but she didn't care to figure it out.

Two men stood apart. One wore midnight black with golden runes along the hems and cuffs, the other wore a gold-colored tunic and trousers.

She stared idly at the young man in gold with a matching turban. His outfit was eye-catching. Prince Something. Xylander. His name was Xylander. She vaguely recalled traveling with him.

214

It slowly dawned on her that he stood beside Joad, who was dressed as a pagan priest. She realized that the runes, or sigils, on the older man's robe were ancient writing. Something was horribly wrong with the priest. She tried to focus. He had grown horns like a goat.

How very odd.

She couldn't dredge up any stronger feeling.

Altar. Pagan priest. Sacrifice.

A voice in Lauryn's mind insisted danger surrounded her.

Evil.

Run far, far away!

But Lauryn's thoughts floated remotely, as if she were watching it happen to somebody else.

A movement in her side vision drew her attention. The prince in gold climbed up the mountain's granite face. He looked like a gold beetle, his hands and feet spread out finding finger and toe holds. Who would climb wearing ceremonial garb?

Surely, she should feel something when he lost his grip and fell several feet before grabbing a jutting rock? But only idle curiosity kept her watching.

He eventually made it to a ledge. Below, a reddish-purple lump lay. At first, she thought it a snake when a head on a long neck raised up. Then the creature's wings flapped as it rose to its full height, larger than a man, and glanced down at the golden boy. It squawked in challenge and thrust its beak at him.

The prince ducked at the last moment, out of its reach.

The bird thrashed around. It caused a boulder to roll down the cliff in its agitation. It trumpeted a cry and struck again with its long, sharp beak. But the golden prince whipped a scimitar up and cut off the bird's head.

Lauryn stood rooted to the ground. She knew she should feel horror but layers of unconcern cocooned her heart from feeling anything. Yet a warm drop of wetness tracked from her eye down her cheek, and she tasted the saltiness of it.

She knew her future was somehow tied up in the violent act.

She blinked the water from her eyes and saw the golden prince standing over the dead bird. He pulled a long tail feather and waved it above his head. The men, who gathered around her, sent up a solemn cheer.

A tail feather. He had killed the magnificent beast for a feather. *Curious.*

Faces flitted before her mind's eye. People she loved. She had let them down somehow. *What was she supposed to do?* Something important. She tried to remember. She tried to care.

Whether a moment passed or an hour, she knew not. The priest suddenly blotted out everything else as he loomed over her. His eyes were pools of darkness, as black as his ceremonial robe. A crown of goat horns sat on his brow. He embodied evil.

Lauryn knew she should be afraid, even terrified. But other than a small part of her mind telling her to run, an icy indifference encased her. And the effort to make her leaden limbs move was beyond her.

Besides, what did it matter? It was too late to do whatever she had come to do. The firebird—for now she knew it was that—was dead.

The six men in the semicircle around her began to chant to a drumbeat. The harsh, guttural sound grated on her nerves. Even in a foreign language the words sounded greedy and bloodthirsty.

"Come, princess. You still have a part to play." The head priest helped her climb upon the granite slab. She laid down at his command. He fastened her wrists and ankles with rope to iron loops as he spoke in a soothing voice. "The prince needs our help. You want to help, don't you? He will be the greatest ruler Canteor has ever seen. Much more powerful than Valdeor's Reina."

Mother. He spoke of her mother.

A tiny tear opened in her heart on hearing Mother's title. Worry and sorrow melted some of the ice surrounding her heart. Mother needed her to fight this lethargy.

"The blood of a pure virgin, and a royal princess at that, will satisfy my master Panmin."

The first frisson of fear ran through her. Her breaths came faster.

Blood.

Sacrifice.

Hers.

Then the golden prince was there, staring at her over the priest's shoulder. "Leave her. Make your preparations, Joad."

The priest tightened his jaw muscles as if he didn't like being ordered about. But he made a sketchy bow and moved away.

The prince fiddled with the knot holding her left hand in place. He slipped something metal into that hand, farthest from the chanting men.

He leaned close and whispered, "I had to go along with Joad's plans, or we wouldn't have left the village alive." Concern etched his face. "You were supposed to agree to our betrothal. Then they would sacrifice the goat. I never meant this to happen. Please believe me."

He brought a handful of crushed leaves to her mouth. "Chew on these and they will counteract the drug."

She opened her mouth and he fed them to her. Her face scrunched up as she chewed the bitter leaves. She swallowed them.

"You must free yourself, Lauryn. When I approach the altar again, that is your signal to run. I will hold them back for as long as I can. But I am only one sword against so many. You must hurry and cut yourself free." He glanced behind him. "I know you can do this." He touched her cheek. "You're the bravest girl I know."

Lauryn stared emptily at the prince's face. Then he moved out of her sight.

Bravest girl he knew.

She didn't feel brave. She felt dull-witted. She had no energy to fight any of this.

Yet she glanced at the object he had given her. A silver dagger. And the hand that held it was free. Even as she registered the futility of trying to escape, surrounded by the enemy, she started sawing the rope around her other hand anyway.

The prince had given her a precious gift. Hope.

15 Holy Pool

*T*wo-stories high arched shrine doors loomed over Allyria and her companions. The thundering waterfall rushed under the bridge behind them.

Beside her, Aunt Donella pulled an iron ring to open a man-size door within the great doors. It was hidden among the carved vines and leaves decorating the larger doors.

Cool air enveloped them as they crossed the threshold. A trinity symbol of colorful interlocking ovals covered the tiled entryway floor. Allyria recognized the seven jeweled tones of the medallion of virtues Mother wore.

Gazing up, she caught her breath at the brilliant stained-glass windows with the sunlight streaming through them.

Allek gasped beside her.

"They depict pilgrims." Aunt Donella ushered them into the main space. She indicated the stained glass above them. "This window shows the lines of people waiting to get inside. See their crutches, bandages, and eye patches?"

Their shoes tapped on the tile floor, echoing in the thick silence, as they moved farther into the room.

Allek spun around, gazing with wonder. "Look! That

man is pouring a pitcher of water onto the arm of a man in a sling." He sucked in his breath. "And below it he stretches out his arm, the sling dropping from his hand."

"And this window depicts a man with an eye patch washing in the pool. The bottom part of the window shows both eyes whole as he points at his head." Allyria clapped her hands.

"These are some of the miracles that took place here. The shrine is ancient; its origins shrouded in mystery. But Uncle Guy and I witnessed similar miracles in our seventeen years of guiding pilgrims here."

"Uncle Guy found the shrine the years the twins were born, didn't he?"

Aunt Donella nodded.

Allek tipped his head way back. "See how high the ceiling is? What an incredible undertaking. How did they manage to get the marble here? And how did they build it so tall? What makes the outside sparkle?"

Aunt Donella's laugh echoed off the walls. "I don't have those answers. But I do know that glass is embedded in the plaster outside which causes it to sparkle in the sun. But how it's stood for a thousand years without any maintenance? Another miracle."

White marble pillars marched like giant trees holding up the vast ceiling. A dais stood in the center of the room, several steps leading up to it.

Aunt Donella led the way to it, after they had their fill of marveling at all the shrine's beautiful details.

A sweet smell pervaded the air. Lily of the valley? It grew stronger as they mounted the steps. An eighteen-inch-high marble wall surrounded a twenty-foot-wide pool of water. Although dust had gathered on the shrine's floor, the water looked pure, clear, and deep.

"No one knows who built the shrine around the healing Waters of Regeneration. But of those who come here, the blind see, the deaf hear, and the lame are made whole." Aunt Donella's reverent tone touched a chord in Allyria's heart. "It also has the power to heal souls. From fear. From despair. Those who visit leave with a greater faith. And it's not only from witnessing miracles. Not all those who visit have physical disabilities."

"Is it true that the water can bring people back to life?" Allek's eyes widened with curiosity.

"Yes. I have seen it happen on a few occasions." Aunt Donella nodded, solemnly.

She picked up a silver mug and dipped it in the waters. She held it out to Allek. "You're allowed to drink, even if there isn't anything wrong with you."

Allek took the mug and gazed at the water a moment before closing his eyes and taking a deep draft.

Wonder passed over his face. He held it out to his sister.

The cold water hit the back of her throat and Allyria shivered at the cool, pure taste.

This ancient building was far removed from the hustle

and bustle and worries of Allyria's everyday life. A strange fancy came over her, making her tingle from head to toe. It was as if she were standing in a place as old as the foundations of the world. She wondered if that's why it was called the Isle of Origin.

Peace, deep and rich, filled every crack of her soul.

Worries slid off of her like a discarded cloak. Fear for Mother's health. Worries about crossing the seas. Anxiety about her own inadequacies.

None of it mattered. If a place like this existed, all life had a purpose. The One Who Fashioned All saw her plight, knew her anxieties. He must truly *care* if He built this place of miracles for them to find.

She imagined she caught a glimpse of the tapestry of life. Birth and growth, love and loss, all woven together in some grand scheme that she couldn't comprehend. But a watchful Creator pulled a thread here, guided a step there. He waited for hearts to call upon Him, to acknowledge Him, so He could pour down His love.

The shrine was imbued with the love of the Creator for his creatures.

Allyria felt renewed in spirit.

She handed the silver mug back. Aunt Donella didn't drink herself. "I've already benefited from their healing properties," she answered Allyria's unspoken question.

Allek retrieved the flask in his pack. He dipped it in the well of water and drew it up. Corking it, he slung the loop over his shoulder.

They exited the shrine and took a path around the outside. At the back, a dormitory and kitchen sat on the remaining cleared ground.

The twins washed up and helped make the meal. Allek drew regular water from a well and carried in a pailful. Allyria busied herself peeling and chopping vegetables that Aunt Donella had her pick from the enclosed garden.

They sat around one of the many tables in the dining area and ate hot vegetable soup. Aunt Donella also served chunks of goat cheese which the island's resident monk provided for the pilgrim's repast. They tried the dragon's blood fruit and some other fruits in a bowl. Allek squirreled away several pieces in his pockets. He fit the definition of a growing boy, always hungry.

"Our resident hermit, Pellas, keeps to himself. I doubt you'll see him while we are here. But he tends the garden and the flock of goats." Aunt Donella gazed into the distance. "Uncle Guy and I ferry fewer pilgrims here each year. I worry sometimes that the barrier around the island will come back. Then it'll once again shroud the island's whereabouts until another age when faith wanes. Only to reappear in order to strengthen men's belief in the Creator."

On the following day, a vessel anchored in the harbor, and a few pilgrims disembarked. Since Aunt Donella was busy tending to them, Allek and Allyria had a chance to explore.

They passed the walled garden. Walking a well-worn path, they found a flock of goats penned in a grassy meadow. The friendly and curious creatures raced over, sniffing for food. Their bleats sounded like a strange laugh, causing Allyria to giggle. Allek whipped out a knife from his pocket and an apple from the other. He cut it up in portions and they fed the goats.

The day after that, they boarded the ship that the pilgrims had arrived on. In their gratitude, the pilgrims had insisted Aunt Donella accompany them when they learned she was on her way to Cressava.

Allyria made friends with some of the youngsters, playing a stone skipping game with them.

Allek, of course, climbed the shrouds to the crow's nest and spent his days up there.

When they came into the harbor of Sikarta, the sailors lowered a dinghy for an older couple that lived there. The first mate took a few men with him and rowed them ashore.

Allyria and her friends hung out at the rail, watching the small boat return. A fin sliced through the waters. Allyria pointed it out gleefully, thinking it was a dolphin. The shark hit the dinghy, nearly toppling it. The first mate fell overboard. Two sailors scrambled to pull him back aboard when he surfaced. Two others smacked the sharp-toothed beast in the nose with their oars, trying to drive it off.

Allyria turned her face from the struggle and prayed.

The sailors were successful at driving off the sea monster. The first mate soon lay on the deck of the ship. His left leg was shredded. Allyria thought his chance of surviving was nonexistent due to the amount of blood leaving his body.

Suddenly, Allek was pushing past her. He carried the flask with the precious water.

Water to heal Mother.

Yet, Allyria couldn't begrudge its use on the injured man.

Allek carefully poured some of the water on the first mate's leg.

As the wound healed, the skin closed up. Allyria let out a breath she didn't realize she was holding in. It resembled the healings depicted in the stained-glass windows. The pale-faced mate sat up, looking with astonishment at his leg, whole again.

She was awestruck. Seeing the miracle in person made her tremble. She had faith in the waters before, but now she truly *believed*.

The pilgrims cheered. The captain and sailors were flabbergasted when they saw the wondrous miracle.

Although happy for him, Allyria's eyes pricked with tears at the thought that his healing might have cost Mother her life. Allyria couldn't imagine a world without Mother.

Later, in the cabin that Aunt Donella and Allyria shared, Aunt Donella praised Allek. "That was quick thinking. I know you worry about your mother and meant it for her. There should still be plenty of the healing waters left for your purpose."

Allyria's heart eased. Part of her wanted to return to the shrine and refill the flask, in case it wasn't enough, but she knew it would only delay them.

The days passed slowly as they sailed back to Cressava. Allyria's anxiety lessened when Aunt Donella decided to shorten their trip. She used Cressava's portal to travel to Bidori island, and from there they jumped to their homeland.

The jump was excruciatingly long. Allyria had severe nausea when they landed back in Valdeor. She heaved until there was no more left inside. Allek gave her a drink of regular water. Aunt Donella made her lie down and rest.

They were in the open along the seacoast somewhere. Allyria watched the seagulls circle overhead, their plaintive cry and the sound of the crash of waves eventually making her drowsy.

When she gradually opened her eyes, she realized that she had slept a long time by the sun's high position.

"Can you make one more trip through the portal?" Aunt Donella's concerned face hovered above her. "Then we can sleep tonight in a town. We'll resume traveling in the morning."

Allyria sat up. Her stomach was no longer threatening to empty itself. She dreaded stepping through the portal again so soon, but she would do it for Mother.

Allek grasped her hand and pulled her to her feet. He kept a hold of her as Aunt Donella activated the worn waypost on the cliff side. Mist rose. When the center cleared, a quiet city appeared.

She nodded her readiness as Aunt Donella quirked an eyebrow at her. Allek squeezed Allyria's fingers, and she followed him through. Aunt Donella brought up the rear.

Allyria waited for her stomach to clench, but it was calm. She stepped onto cobblestones, releasing a big sigh. The waypost was in front of a stable.

The sun was below the roofs of the town, a soft twilight descending on them.

"A fire destroyed the inn that once stood here. Come, I know a place we can stay the night."

They followed Aunt Donella, who led them down the street. Two-story wooden buildings towered above them. They traversed the main thoroughfare, and then she turned down a side street.

"Are all wayposts connected to inns?" Allek asked.

"Many are. It's because they were once stops for the pilgrims. Waykeepers offered rest areas and food. Inns naturally sprung up to cater to the travelers. Then the Waykeepers dwindled in numbers, the wayposts were forgotten, and only the inns remained."

Lights shone through windows of a large building. The sign outside proclaimed it the Jolly Seadog. Two men exited, allowing the homey scent of roast beef to waft out. Beside

Allyria, Allek's stomach grumbled. Her own stomach clenched with hunger. When was the last time she ate?

Soon the three were seated in the dining area, hot meat pies dripping with gravy on the plates before them. Allyria washed her first bite down with cool butterscotch beer.

The taste of it reminded her of home. Even though they were almost there, sharp pains of homesickness pierced her. She missed Mother and Father. She missed Lysa and her older siblings. She missed a warm bath and her soft bed. She was ready for this adventure to be over.

Walking back to the waypost the next morning, Allyria saw the giant watchtower that she couldn't discern last night in the dark. It could only mean that they had landed in Tulken Harbor on the southern coast. Their destination, the palace at Mintala, was in central Valdeor.

"I'm going to take you through three portals. If you feel sick, let me know and we'll rest." Aunt Donella's gaze rested on Allyria. "Otherwise, we should be back to the palace by this afternoon."

They stepped through the stable's portal and ended up in a small clearing in the woods. Gnarled, old-growth trees pressed around them. The oppressive air dripped with humidity and smelled of sweet, rotten vegetation.

Allyria had a bad feeling about this place. Even Allek seemed reluctant to explore the menacing area.

From there, they went to a rock house made of giant slabs in a valley. The cozy dwelling and tiny garden had a welcome feeling to it, the opposite of the last place.

"This was Usher's house. He mentored me and Uncle Guy." Seeing Allyria's pale face, Aunt Donella insisted that they rest while she made Allyria a cup of tea.

Entering the dwelling, Aunt Donella reached for herbs hanging from the ceiling. She sent Allek to fill an old, black pot with water from a spring. She added the herbs and put them to boil.

Allek poked all around the room, studying the stone slabs, asking Aunt Donella what she knew about the place.

"It's ancient. Even Usher didn't know its history."

"What a feat of engineering. I wonder if they used pulleys to put the stones in place. They must each weigh a ton or more. It looks like giants built it." By the look in Allek's eyes, Allyria could tell the building impressed her twin.

"That's what Usher said when I met him." Aunt Donella chuckled.

Allyria sat at the table on one of two chairs. She gazed around the snug room with a pot over the fire, a bed tucked in the corner with a cheerful quilt, and shelves with mugs and dishes stacked neatly in place. The hanging herbs tickled her nose with their pungent scents. The stone dwelling should've been cold, but the homey touches made it feel cozy. It still bore the imprint of the previous owner.

While they sipped the warm tea, Aunt Donella regaled

them with stories of Usher training her. Whatever was in the drink, comforted Allyria's stomach.

"Who gave the portals their magic?" Allek fiddled with a mortar and pestle that Aunt Donella had used to crush the herbs.

"The Guardian of Valdeor, servant of the One Who Fashioned All, placed the portals. It is through his power that we are transported. Some travelers say they feel as if someone grabs them by the hair when they make the jump from waypost to waypost. And some, like my husband Guy, have actually seen and spoken to the being made of light."

"Wow! That's awesome. I hope I see him someday." Allek abandoned the marble utensils. "When I travel through the portal, I feel as if I'm flying in a dark tunnel."

"The Guardian doesn't appear unless he has a message from the Most High, so if you see him, it will be because you are called to do something momentous."

Allek looked thoughtful.

"Mother saw him on two occasions." Allyria put down her mug and leaned forward. "Once when he gave her a long life, and the other time, a hundred years later, when he declared her Reina over Valdeor."

She wondered how Mother had felt on those occasions. A being made of pure light? Mother said the Guardian seemed to sift through her very thoughts and knew her heart.

The Guardian sounded glorious, yet fearsome, to Allyria.

When they approached the portal after that, calm settled over Allyria. The Guardian wouldn't let anything bad befall her since he served the Most High.

16 Sacrifice

auryn!" a familiar voice shouted with raw emotion.

Her distraught glance searched the area. Two men struggled with two others as they moved from the mountain ledge toward the tent. She caught Everard's terrified gaze. Not for himself, but fear for her. Time seemed to slow as something intense passed between them.

If Ever was here, her brothers were sure to be here, too. She saw Allyn detained with him, but no sign of Jarell. Both young men stared at her with horror as they took in her situation.

Lauryn struggled to manipulate the dagger to cut the rope around her right wrist without detection.

Whatever drug they had given her had begun to wear off the longer she worked. Terror seeped its way through her body, giving her the jolt she needed. She desperately wanted to live.

Please help me, O Thou who Fashioned All! Guide my hand. Keep the others safe!

How could she have thought deceiving her brother was the way to win a crown? She deserved to lose after putting her trust in Xylander, an outsider, over her twin. She had known what Allyn and Ever would've said about going off alone with the Canteor prince, yet she had silenced her conscience. And now she might pay with her life!

While she secretly hacked at the stiff rope, she reluctantly drew her eyes away from Ever and Allyn. She cast her gaze around the clearing, assessing how much time she had before someone noticed her.

Three men brought wood and stacked it in the bird's nest. Chanting, Joad set a torch to the pyre. They must've soaked the wood in pitch, for flames whooshed ten feet high.

The injustice caused her eyes to prick with tears.

As soon as they finished with the bird, she knew their attention would turn to her.

Too quickly for her needs, the light and warmth from the burning pyre diminished.

Freeing her right hand, she sent up a thanksgiving prayer. She nearly sat up to tackle her feet until she saw Joad heading to the altar where she lay. No way she could free herself before he arrived. She tucked the dagger under her right hand, hoping he'd overlook it as his eyes adjusted from the bright firelight.

Fear trickled down her spine. She rearranged the ropes to drape over her hands before Joad towered over her. She wiped her face of expression, staring at a point over his shoulder.

The six chanting men from earlier assembled in a loose

ring around the altar's perimeter, whether to keep her in or others out, she didn't know.

Joad stretched up his right hand, holding a ceremonial blade which glinted in the pyre's light. He began swaying, singing a soft chant. His voice slowly grew in volume. He spoke words in a language foreign to Lauryn, but they sounded guttural, conjuring darkness. She could feel a miasma of evil settling over the altar.

Sweat beaded over her body as she was gripped with fear.

In the distance, she could hear Allyn and Ever yelling.

Her limbs shook and terror pumped through her veins as Joad called down his pagan god to witness her sacrifice. She gripped the dagger with a damp, slippery hand as she waited for a sign from Xylander.

Please, please, please.

A movement caught her gaze. She saw Xylander draw closer as Joad reached the climax, the priest's blade descending. Xylander swung his scimitar and pierced Joad's side, abruptly silencing him. Joad's body fell across her, his dagger flying out of his hand.

A second of shocked silence followed, then chaos erupted as several men leapt at Xylander, weapons drawn. He held them off, becoming a whirlwind of deadly, slashing motion.

A whoop sounded. Jarell, Irdek and his men swarmed from behind rocks around the perimeter.

The knot in her chest loosened somewhat. Help had come!

Her eyes sought out Ever. His face suffused with rage as he used the confusion to break free. He grappled with his captor for the man's sword, then used it to slash the nearest worshiper that stood between her and him.

Lauryn dragged her gaze away from the fighting, heaved Joad's body off her and sat up. She frantically reached for the rope tying her feet. Working as fast as she could, she sliced free. The knife slipped and made a small gash in her ankle. She ignored the welling blood and slipped from the slab. She stumbled. She wasn't sure if her sudden lightheadedness came from the drug or the day's events.

Her gaze fell on a dead man holding a knife in its outstretched hand. She fought down a gagging reflex as she retrieved the weapon. She grasped it in her left hand.

Now armed with two weapons, she gazed around looking for someone to attack.

Xylander left a trail of bodies behind him. He currently held his own against three men.

Halfway across the space to the altar, Ever and Jarell fought back-to-back. A dozen of Irdek's men fought those in black robes.

A cry sounded behind her and she spun around. Allyn held his sword in one hand and a burning branch from the pyre in the other. His foe's robe lit on fire. The man wildly beat it with his bare hands.

Then she saw Giada standing alone at the fray's edge. The boys could handle themselves so she raced toward her friend.

Her ears were filled with the sounds of the attack—clashing of weapons, grunts and cries of the injured.

Three men had also spied Giada and converged on her. Lauryn wouldn't reach the younger girl in time.

Giada used her dagger in a defensive move, giving Lauryn time to act. Blocking out all other sounds, Lauryn stopped and concentrated on her breathing. She braced her feet, and flung the silver dagger that Xylander had given her. It hit the man squarely in the back. Crying out, he dropped.

Not waiting to see what the other two would do, Lauryn ran.

Giada hunched strangely, then threw something black at the other man. A yowl and a man's high scream as he clawed something on his face, let Lauryn know Giada had used Mystic, the jagwaro cub, as a weapon.

The third man raised his arm to strike. Giada swung her dagger up to block it. Lauryn pushed Giada out of the way. She couldn't fully deflect the sword coming at her from that angle. Her forearm stung as the blade nicked it. Lauryn ignored the wound, hardly feeling it as she ducked under the man's arm and buried the other knife in his belly. He clutched it and dropped to the ground.

She turned her eyes away from the gory sight, checking on Giada. Mystic twined around the younger girl's legs.

Heart racing, she took a stand next to her friend. She scanned for further threats. Relief washed over her as she realized that they had won the day.

Lauryn's gaze roamed the area to see how her brothers and Everard had fared. She picked out Jarell speaking with Irdek and his Nyrmidions.

She clasped hands with Giada and pulled her toward them as she searched for the others. They spotted Allyn on the firebird's ledge.

Giada left her and climbed up the cliff to join Allyn, who stood over the smoldering pyre of ashes, what was left of the mighty firebird. Their faces reflected the sorrow Lauryn felt at the loss of the bird.

Xylander scrambled up to the other side of the nest on the ledge.

Flames suddenly shot up, and her twin jumped back, pulling Giada with him.

The plain grew eerily silent as something moved in the dark flames. A thin head poked out, then wings spread wide. A haunting cry shivered in Lauryn's soul as the firebird sang.

Xylander must've made a movement because the firebird squawked and stumbled out of the flames, away from his bright gold silhouette. Then Mystic pounced, stalking it. Retreating from the jagwaro, the firebird tripped and fell against Allyn. Her brother reached out to touch it and the firebird let him. It hunched placidly at his feet as if it were a pet.

Allyn plucked a feather.

The bird let out a trumpeting sound as if she were scolding them all, then rose into the air and flew away. No one said a word, watching the majestic purple bird disappear into the clouds.

Lauryn glanced at her twin, who dropped his gaze from the retreating firebird to the feather in his hand, a look of wonder on his face.

Allyn had won the quest!

Lauryn should feel disappointment but she was too thankful to be alive. Only moments ago, she had cheated death.

Her eye caught movement. Everard strode over to Lauryn, sheathing his sword. He wrapped his arms around her and pulled her against his chest. She threw her arms around his waist. She relaxed her head against his shoulder and breathed in his familiar scent of leather and citrus.

"I thought you were going to die! I've never been so afraid in my life," he whispered as he held her tight.

She pulled back enough to smile up at him. "I know... You can't live without me."

A sudden movement at his back drew her eye. "EVER!"

A bloody Joad staggered and swung the ceremonial dagger at them. Ever roughly pushed her away. The dagger pierced his back.

"NO!" She screamed and caught him as he fell forward. His weight was too much, pushing her down until she sprawled on a rock, holding his limp body.

Lauryn's mind froze in shock.

Jarell suddenly appeared, cutting down Joad.

Ever gazed longingly at Lauryn with his deep hazel eyes and gasped, "At least you're safe, Laurie." His face paled even further and his eyes grew unfocused.

Her heart squeezed with intense pain. "Stay with me, Ev! You can't die! I never told you that I love you!" Tears blurred her sight of him.

Shaking, she pulled Guy's ring from around her neck. She caught Allyn's horrified gaze across the clearing. He nodded as she slipped the ring on.

Mist pooled around her feet. She grasped Ever's dead weight against her chest. Then it was as if a hand grabbed the top of her head and transported her and her burden through a portal.

She heard a wailing cry in the dark and realized it came from her own throat.

17 Mintala

Arriving at the garden gate portal in the palace courtyard, where Allyria and Allek had started from, Hallett, a member of the royal guard assigned to the twins, met them. He showed signs of relief.

"Your Highnesses, I have been stationed here, waiting for you. The king desires your presence, immediately."

Allyria's chest tightened. How much trouble were they in? Yet, even if Father punished her, it would be worth it if the water healed Mother.

Hallett swept before them. Allek grabbed Allyria's hand, and squeezed it reassuringly. Hallett led them through the side door away from the family wing. He stopped before the throne room. The guards stationed outside gave them a cursory glance.

Hallett rapped on the door and stepped back.

"Enter," Allyria heard Father call.

Stiffening her spine, she hurried across the threshold. Father stood up from his seat as his gaze fell upon them. Courtiers and petitioners all turned to stare at them.

Allyria's cheeks grew warm. Their behavior would be

the fodder of gossip for months to come.

Father ordered everyone from the room. Forgetting all decorum, Allyria crossed the space and threw herself at him when they were alone. His arms closed around her.

"Oh, Father! It's good to be home. You mustn't be mad at Allek. It was my idea! He only came to protect me." Allyria gushed, words tumbling out. "We brought water for Mother. From the Isle of Origin."

"Allyria, calm yourself."

She looked up into his face with its stern expression, but his eyes softened as he touched her cheek.

Allek came to stand beside her. "It's not all her fault, no matter what she says. I wanted to go, too. To the island. To find a cure for Mother."

Father briefly put his hand on Allek's shoulder and squeezed.

Father dropped his hand. They straightened to attention at his expression.

"Your mother and I were worried, until we heard that Donella was with you."

Allyria glanced back, but Aunt Donella wasn't there. She had left them to face Father on their own.

Father crossed his arms. "Tell me the story from the beginning. You start Allyria, since you say it was your idea."

And so she told him how they thought the waters might heal Mother, and how they thought no one would listen to their ideas, and how they set off to acquire it for themselves.

"We brought back the Water of Regeneration for Mother." Allek retrieved the flask, hanging on a strap over his shoulder and held it out to Father.

"The healing waters won't work for me."

At the familiar voice, Allyria spun to see two royal guards carrying Mother in a chair through the side door. They placed her chair next to the throne, Trekker III on their heels.

"Mother!" Allyria ran and threw herself at Mother's feet, hugging her knees. She was afraid to embrace Mother tightly, afraid of hurting her.

A gentle hand rubbed her hair. "While I appreciate your willingness to find a cure, if you had asked, I would've told you that I already drank from the Water of Regeneration."

Allyria pulled back her head where it rested on Mother's knees to look at her lovely, worn face.

"You did?" Allyria's heart plunged, cold spreading through her chest.

Allek joined them, sitting on the chair's arm. Mother wrapped an arm around him.

"I visited the shrine when Guy first found it. That was a month after our first set of twins were born. Their birth had sapped my strength. I was one hundred and twenty-one years old then. I felt like my time was coming to an end. My heirs would have to fulfill my legacy. In fact, I was sorrowful at the time. Afraid I wouldn't see them grow up." Tears stood in her eyes.

Father came to put his arm around Mother. She leaned into him.

"Then I drank the water from the holy pool. Strength poured into me. I knew I would live many more years. I prayed I would have more children. I'm so blessed in all of my babies." She brushed Allyria's hair back with her fingers.

"But why won't it work again?" Allek spoke the question in Allyria's mind. "If it's so powerful, can't it extend your life?"

"I have lived far longer than any other person. I'm fairly certain I'll see the twins' eighteenth birthday, but I'm not guaranteed any days beyond that."

Tears dripped down Allyria's cheeks. Mother brushed them away.

"I'm not afraid to go to the One Who Fashioned All's loving arms." Mother glanced from one to the other. "When the time comes, I want you to be happy for me. I'll ask Him to comfort you and hold you in the palms of His hands." She laid a hand on Allek's head when his face screwed up as he tried to hold back his grief.

Allyria's heart broke.

Trekker's cold nose pushed her hand, as if he sensed her sorrow.

Before she could say anything, the main doors of the room crashed open. Trekker III barked. Uncle Guy rushed in, Aunt Donella in his wake. "They're coming home!"

Mist swirled in the center of the throne room near the

pedestal with the diamond heartstone. Light crackled, causing the heartstone gems in the embrasures above their heads to glow with red and green, blue and orange, yellow and purple lights.

Lauryn appeared, sitting on a boulder with Prince Everard slumped in her lap. A dagger's hilt stuck out of his back.

Allyria heard others gasp with her as she gazed with horror on the scene. Before anyone could move or speak, more mist formed at the other end of the room. Allyn staggered out of it, Jarell clutching his brother's shoulder and a girl grasping Allyn's hand. In his other hand, Allyn held his bloodied sword. All three of them were spattered with blood, as well.

Lauryn's voice broke the frozen tableau. "Help! Ever is dying!"

Allyria stared with shock at Prince Everard. His pale face, limp figure, and blood at the corner of his mouth seemed to indicate that he was already dead, or very near it.

Father rushed to take Everard's weight from Lauryn, whose white dress was soaked in blood.

Mother tried to stand, but sank back in her chair. "Quick, Allek, Allyria! Use the water."

Allyria blinked. Then she followed Allek as he picked up the flask at his feet and ran, uncorking it as he went.

"Step back!" Allyria commanded as Uncle Guy, Aunt Donella, Allyn, Jarell, and the blond-haired girl converged on Lauryn and Everard.

Light exploded around Lauryn. She tilted backward with Ever's weight pressing on her.

She noticed that the white robe the Panmin fanatics had forced on her was stained red with Ever's blood. Her stomach threatened to revolt. Tears closed her throat and stung her eyes as she stared at her beloved's deathly pale face. He wasn't breathing.

Her grief was a throbbing ache in her chest.

No! It couldn't end like this. She didn't want him to die for her. She wanted him at her side. Forever.

She was vaguely aware of other people surrounding them. Ever needed a physician before he bled out. She cried for help.

Then Father was there, easing her burden.

Everyone came running, but Allek pushed through the concerned onlookers. He carried a flask.

Ever didn't need a drink! He needed a physician. Didn't anyone else understand that he was dying?

"The dagger, Father!" Allek's eyes were confident.

Father's expression changed from sorrowful to hopeful. He nodded at Allek and yanked out the dagger from Everard's back.

Lauryn screamed.

Father laid Everard's still body face down on the floor.

Allek leaned over Everard and steadily poured water over the wound.

Stunned, Lauryn watched as the gash healed up. Ever took a shallow breath, then a deeper one. He groaned and rolled over on his back.

Lauryn fell on her knees beside him as he blinked.

"Ever! You're alive!" She gulped her sobs back.

He reached for her hand and she clasped it.

"Are you hurt, Laurie?" anxiety laced his voice as he focused on her bloody dress.

"No. It's your blood, not mine. You saved me." With her free hand, she brushed away the tears that kept falling.

Father helped Everard to sit up.

"Good. I'd die for you."

"You did!" Her emotions were all over the place as she drank in the sight of him alive. She couldn't let go of his hand, clinging to him as if her happiness depended on it. "Allek somehow brought you back to life."

Looking up at her youngest brother, she choked out, "I don't know what you did, but thank you, Allek! You really are an angel."

Allyria squeezed in beside him, grinning from ear to ear. "Allek and I journeyed to the Isle of Origin and brought back the Water of Regeneration. We meant it for Mother, but she said it wouldn't help her."

Her heart slowing to normal, Lauryn took stock of the situation. She was in the throne room of her home, surrounded by her family and Giada, Guy, and Donella. Everyone began talking at once.

"Does anyone need a physician?" Father's voice cut over the chatter. When they found most of them had minor scrapes and cuts, Father ordered Hallett, who was hovering in the background, to summon the royal physician.

Father sent a servant to the kitchen to order food prepared for the travelers.

"Once you have all been looked over, I want you to go to your rooms and clean up. We can reconvene in the small dining hall and you can tell your stories."

The physician, an older man who had delivered all the siblings, examined Allyn, Jarell, Lauryn and Giada. Everard insisted he go last since the water healed him. Allyn and Jarell had some nasty cuts, none life-threatening.

Lauryn, in the excitement, had forgotten the gash on her arm. Giada's life was worth the minor injury Lauryn had incurred when she pushed Giada out of the way. And she hardly felt a sting on her ankle caused by the slip of Xylander's knife.

When the physician finished binding Lauryn's arm, she put her good arm around Giada and led her to her suite. Maids had already laid a hot bath. Lauryn coaxed Giada into soaking first.

Lauryn laid down on her bed, meaning to rest for a moment while waiting for her turn. A hand gently shook Lauryn awake. Giada was dressed, standing beside the bed.

"I'd let you sleep, but the newly-filled bath will get cold."

Lauryn sighed with delight as her sore body submerged into the warm water. Although she could soak for a day in the soothing bathwater, Lauryn made herself leave it, dress, and comb her hair. Giada braided the wet locks for her, then they went downstairs to the small dining room.

Mother sat at the head of the table. Lauryn hugged her carefully. Mother kissed her forehead. "Welcome home, darling."

Giada made a deep curtsy. Mother clasped Giada's hands when she arose. "Giada, I didn't recognize you at first."

Giada blushed, touching her short curls.

Lysa appeared out of nowhere and tightly held onto Lauryn. "Lauryn, I missed you so much!"

"Hey, there, Sweetie-pie! Have you been a good girl?" Lysa chattered about the books she had read to Mother, while she dragged Lauryn by the hand to the food set out.

Lauryn hadn't realized how hungry she was until she smelled warm ham slices baked in cinnamon and other spices. She forked some on her plate along with sweet potatoes and a chunk of fresh-baked bread.

Father called for order when Lauryn, Allyn, Jarell, Lysa, Allyria, Allek, Giada, Everard, Guy and Donella all sat at the table with heaping plates.

"Eat your fill, then Lauryn can tell her tale. Allyn will follow. Allyria will have a turn last as she may clear up the mystery that is bothering Everard. Of course, our guests Guy and Donella can add details where the narrative is lacking. As can Jarell and Everard."

Lauryn couldn't take her time savoring the food because the desire to satisfy everyone's curiosity, including her own, weighed on her.

But as she began to speak, a servant announced Prince Gensard of Samarantha. He strode into the room, his wife, Princess Jiana, trailing behind him. He looked around the table until his eyes found his daughter.

"Giada! How could you do this to us? Your mother has been prostrated with anxiety. Have you no care for her feelings?"

Lauryn saw Giada quail under his stern expression. Giada glanced apologetically at her mother who looked wan. Princess Jiana's face brightened at the sight of her daughter well and whole.

Giada squared her shoulders and lifted her chin, less in defiance, more as if she gathered her courage. "I'm sorry I upset Mother. I shouldn't have gone, but in the end, my part was invaluable in saving Lauryn."

Mother forestalled Prince Gensard. "We are about to hear the details of the quest we sent the twins on. I see you received the message we sent through the portal that your daughter arrived safely. You are welcome to join us. Please partake of the food, if you wish."

Prince Gensard's jaw tightened, as if he held in what he wanted to say. Instead, he pulled out a chair for his wife and sat. Although his expression as he stared at Giada promised his lecture wasn't forgotten but only postponed.

Lauryn told her audience about Prince Xylander joining them in Samarantha. Aunt Donella remarked that it had been Mother's desire to include him. Lauryn faltered, giving Mother a questioning glance. But as Mother motioned for her to continue, Lauryn described the separation that happened when they used the portal to travel to Hamleor.

Prince Gensard made a noise when he heard how Giada joined moments before their catastrophic break. But at a look from Mother, he subsided. He crossed his arms and glared at his daughter.

Lauryn went on to tell how they met Irdek, and Everard's eventual appearance.

"He joined you at my request. I didn't know his great-grandmother was dying," Father interposed. "Although I wanted to send a squadron with you to keep you safe, I knew Everard would lay down his life for either of you." Father's gaze landed on Everard. "Apparently I was proven right."

As Lauryn described Captain Yeager abducting her, Father's eyes narrowed. "We recently received the ransom note from this self-styled pirate king."

Her parents seemed relieved to learn how Ever and Xylander had come to her rescue.

"But Prince Xylander kept the firebird's whereabouts

secret. I know, now, that he had his own reasons for doing so. But he would've saved us a lot of trouble if he'd been forthcoming from the beginning."

Lauryn had mixed feelings when it came to Xylander. He'd eventually helped get them to the right port in Canteor. But anger still burned inside her that he'd convinced her to travel alone with him that morning. What had he done the previous day in Caervale? Could he have met with the followers of Panmin? Did he really not know the supposed guides were worshipers of the false god? How could he endanger her life if he cared for her? So many questions. Yet he was no longer with them to answer them.

She refocused when she noticed everyone had finished eating and was waiting for her to continue.

She mentioned reuniting with her brothers and the journey to Canteor. She gave the details on the subsequent run-in with the Panmin fanatics and Xylander's shocking proposal.

Everard, sitting next to her, made a sound of disgust.

Lauryn's heart sped up reciting her near-death experience.

Ever reached under the table and squeezed her hand. Her anxiety bled out at the comforting touch.

She turned to Allyn. "I should've never left with Xylander. Even if it were a competition, we should've faced it together. Being captured was my own fault. I'm responsible for the wounds you received trying to save me." Her shame dug deep. "Can you ever forgive me, Allyn? And you, too?" She glanced at Everard, Jarell and Giada.

"Of course. You've always been our leader," Allyn declared, his eyes earnest. "We would follow you anywhere."

Even though he said that, she sensed a difference in him. From what she had observed, he was the leader of his group. He had a new air of confidence about him. He'd had to make hard decisions, and it showed.

"My sword is yours to command." Everard seconded the sentiment. His gaze rested on her warmly.

"You saved my life! There's nothing to forgive," Giada exclaimed.

Giada explained to her parents and the gathering how Lauryn had jumped in front of the sword meant for her. Her mother and father gasped.

Lauryn, embarrassed by Giada's heroine-worship, protested that the cut on her arm was slight.

"What ever happened to your jagwaro, Giada?" Jarell changed the conversation. A quick glance at her brother, seeing his wink, let Lauryn know he had done it on purpose. When had he become so diplomatic?

"In the rush, I had to leave Mystic behind." Giada's eyes teared up. She described how the cat's last action saved her. The jagwaro scratched her attacker's face when she threw Mystic at him.

"You had a-a *jagwaro* as a pet?" Princess Jiana's astonishment had the younger generation laughing.

"A big kitten, Mama. Even you wouldn't be afraid of it."

Conversations sprang up around the table now that Lauryn had finished her explanation.

Lauryn glanced around at her brothers and friends. Gratitude filled her heart. They forgave her! She choked down a burning sensation at the back of her throat. She wouldn't cry in front of everyone.

She'd been selfish. Not a leader's trait. And yet they still believed in her. She was humbled by their faith in her.

She promised herself she'd live up to their trust in her, with the Most High's help.

18 The Heir

When the talk died down, Allyn took up the tale. "Giada came at my bidding. I welcomed her into our circle."

He knew in his heart that if he hadn't glanced back and smiled at her, she wouldn't have dared come. In his selfishness, he had wanted her to see him prove himself a man. One worthy to sit on the throne of the high king.

Shame at his error washed through him as he glanced at Princess Jiana who showed signs of prolonged grief. Dark circles were under her eyes even as she clasped Giada's hand in hers. She looked thinner and more careworn than the last time they had gathered together in Samarantha.

Allyn met Prince Gensard's frown and intense stare with trepidation.

Although he had solemnly guarded Giada from danger as best as he could, he shouldn't have put her there in the first place.

His feelings for Giada made it worse. After his recklessness with her safety, Prince Gensard had every right to deny him the chance to court Giada when she was old enough.

Mother gave him a searching look, as if she could read his heart. And maybe she could. She often knew or guessed their secrets.

Allyn hurried on. He tried to gloss over the danger Giada faced in the alleyway of Oster. But Giada's father wouldn't have it. He demanded details from Giada and corroboration from Jarell.

"So that's why you cut your hair and are dressed like a boy." Prince Gensard huffed. He didn't seem pleased that Allyn had taught her to defend herself either.

Princess Jiana was more sympathetic. "It's a hard, cruel world. We have, perhaps, sheltered you too much from it." She leaned over and hugged her daughter. At her gentle rebuke, Prince Gensard seemed to pause, his expression softening as he met his wife's eyes.

"We have endeavored to raise our girls, as well as boys, to defend themselves." Father smiled at Giada, then caught her father's gaze. "Yes, we have guards with our children at all times, but we've never underestimated their need to watch out for themselves. We royals remain targets as you know, Gensard."

Prince Gensard gave a small nod of agreement, reluctantly.

The knot in Allyn's gut loosened.

With the tension eased, Allyn resumed telling them about finding the mirror pool and fighting the giant salamander. "And if it weren't for Giada, the trip to the cave would've been wasted. She was the one who saw the vision of the firebird's location."

Giada's parents glanced at her, a proud light in their eyes.

Allyn swallowed. He dreaded their reaction to their run-in with the mighty storm and nearly drowning. But all the parents seemed resigned to the dangers at this point in the story.

Allyn mentioned meeting Irdek and reuniting with Lauryn.

Allyn wound up with his suspicions about Xylander's motives in all of this. "The last I saw of the Canteor prince, he was astride a horse, ordering Irdek to round up the survivors."

"He's like a cat." Lauryn drummed her fingers on the table.

"Because he has nine lives?" Jarell asked.

"That too. But I was thinking he always lands on his feet." Lauryn met Allyn's gaze. He nodded in agreement.

Mother reiterated that it was her idea to include Xylander. "Once I heard that he was visiting Samarantha, I thought it a perfect chance for you and Lauryn to get to know the crown prince. Under trying circumstances, you might forge a powerful friendship. Your generation could cement ties between our lands, or develop more lasting connections." Her gaze landed on Lauryn, who blushed. "But after all that happened, I'm not surprised you refused his offer of marriage."

"I still can't work out if Xylander meant to betray me— us, or was reluctantly on our side." Lauryn glanced between Allyn and Everard seemingly not trusting her own assessment of him.

"Betray you," Everard bit out.

"Work with us," Allyn said simultaneously.

Catching the surprised looks of everyone, Allyn gathered his thoughts. "I didn't trust him, initially. I don't entirely trust him now. But Xylander did give you the means to escape, Lauryn."

"After putting her in a deadly situation," Everard countered.

Glancing surreptitiously at Giada, who caught his glance and gave him a look of encouragement, Allyn lifted his chin. "I am guilty of the same thing with Giada. I shouldn't have encouraged her to come with us." He sighed.

"Xylander found himself surrounded by a group of his subjects who were misguided adorers of Panmin," Allyn continued. "I'm guessing, Xylander saw himself as a great leader. Who was he to abuse them of their wishes to guarantee him the kingdom through their ceremonial sacrifices? It was only supposed to be the firebird and the goat. But once he realized the danger to Lauryn through his selfish desires, he seemed to do what he could to make amends. He killed as many worshipers—if not more than

Jarell, Ever and I—although they were his subjects. He ended up putting Lauryn's life first."

"Only after he plucked a feather from the firebird and then killed it." Lauryn said dryly.

She swallowed. "I never congratulated you on winning the competition. You'll make a fine king. You made better decisions than I did."

Allyn blinked with surprise at her humbleness.

"Except dragging my daughter on your expedition." Allyn's gut clenched at the thundercloud look Prince Gensard gave him.

Giada's father turned on her, now that he knew the whole story. "You've ruined your reputation gallivanting over two continents with the princes. Your chances at making a good marriage alliance are next to nothing."

Princess Jiana laid her hand on his arm in an effort to calm him. "It sounds as if the Most High had a purpose for her inclusion."

Allyn drew himself up. "Since you bring it up, I wish to make a formal petition to court your daughter."

Giada blinked away her tears, her face brightening as she gazed at him with admiration and something more.

Father and Mother exclaimed. "Allyn—"

"It's my fault her reputation is ruined." Allyn had to make them understand. "Nothing happened. I treated her as if she were my own sister. But if she—"

Mother cut across him. "If you are to be the crown

prince, heir to the throne, you must consider an alliance with other nations. You cannot declare for Giada. Your father and I will discuss this with you later."

Allyn longed to say that in less than two weeks, he'd be eighteen. Surely, he had the right to decide his future queen when he reached his majority. He squashed his defiant thoughts, for the moment. In his mind he knew his parents were right. But his heart balked at letting Giada go.

Tensions ran high in the room.

Allyn backed off. For now. He wouldn't let Giada suffer for his sin. He'd make his parents and her father see reason. In two years she would be eighteen. Prince Gensard might be overprotective, but Allyn thought he had his daughter's best interest at heart. Whether Allyn was ruler of Valdeor, or simply a prince, he knew he was a matrimonial catch of the first order. The prince of Samarantha would see that eventually. He hoped.

Allyn was amazed by Allyria and Allek, who took turns telling of their adventure. He and Lauryn commended their courage. Everard could hardly speak his thanks, seemingly overcome with emotion.

When everyone had had their chance to speak, Mother took over the proceedings. "Now that we have heard your tales, the travelers must rest. I'll call the Council of Nobles to gather in the throne room tomorrow, at high noon. You will give them an abbreviated account of your quest. Then we will make the formal announcement of the next heir."

Father called for the chair bearers. They picked up Mother's chair by poles through slots and carried her away to her chamber.

Although Allyn wanted a moment alone with Giada, her parents whisked her away before he could speak to her. As she passed through the door, she sent Allyn a sorrowful glance.

Allyn's shoulders slumped. They'd have no more time alone together. Her father would see to that.

His only chance at a marriage alliance with her seemed to be if he proved himself a man of virtue to her father. He scrubbed his hand over his face. Virtuous? He'd messed up lots of times on the quest.

He woke early the next morning. Deciding he wouldn't get back to sleep, he thought he'd rid himself of his excess energy on the training field. After a bout with one of the senior guards, he walked back to the palace, deep in thought. He was surprised to see Giada slip into the gardens.

He picked up his pace and followed her into the rose garden.

"Giada!"

She swung around. But she stepped away from him, conflict in her eyes.

Guilt swamped him. She must've endured a severe lecture.

"I'm so sorry I got you into trouble with your father." He ran a hand through his hair. "My intention was never to harm you. I didn't think of your reputation. I mean, Lauryn was supposed to be there with us."

"I chose to go." She dropped her eyes, scuffing the pebbled path with her foot. "You aren't responsible for what happened."

"Of course, I am. But I'll set everything right." He put his hands on her shoulders. "I'll speak privately with your father. He must listen to his high king. We'll get engaged and that will stop people from talking."

"I don't want that, Allyn." She glanced up at him, tears in her eyes.

His heart dropped into his stomach. He thought she'd felt the same as he did. Searching her eyes, he saw regret. "You don't want to marry me someday?" A band tightened around his chest as he dropped his hands to his side.

"I—I can't do this, Allyn." She sobbed and ran away.

A hollow ache spread out from his chest.

But he didn't have time to wallow in his sudden grief. His siblings burst into view and dragged him off to breakfast. Glancing around the table and listening to the lively banter, he realized how much he had missed his family.

When Everard showed up, he was welcomed as one of them, especially by Lauryn. She assured herself that he was doing well before she went back to eating. They kept glancing at each other over the heads of the younger siblings.

A pang of envy went through Allyn at their looming happy ending. He pushed it deep down. He was genuinely glad for them.

All too soon, it was time to gather in the throne room.

Allyn looked around and saw Uncle Guy, Aunt Donella, Prince Gensard, Princess Jiana and Giada had joined them. The Council of Nobles were also present, sitting on benches along the wall.

Father sat on the throne, Trekker III at his feet. Mother was beside him on her movable chair. She motioned Allyn and Lauryn forward and they bowed before the thrones.

They gave accounts of their actions on the quest before the council. Once again, they each donned Mother's medallion, and the stones of virtue gleamed brighter for them than the last time.

Then Allyn reached into the satchel he brought and retrieved the feather he'd taken from the firebird. Mother and Father examined it. Then they passed it to the gathered nobles. They all exclaimed over it.

Mother dipped her head. "Allyn successfully completed the quest. He is Valdeor's crown prince. We will officially declare his succession at his eighteenth birthday celebration."

Shock rolled through him. He knew he was unworthy.

Did the feather signal a worthy leader as Xylander had said? Canteor potentates wore it in their turbans. Did it have a special meaning?

The firebird's feather secured his place as crown prince of Valdeor. One day he'd rule the land!

He caught Lauryn's stare. Her disappointment was palpable. Guilt dug it's claws into him. She deserved this more than he did. She'd worked her whole life for this recognition. He felt like an interloper.

He bowed to Mother and stepped back to the foot of the dais.

"How did this get here?" Jarell's voice drew all eyes to him. He stood near the pedestal at the room's center. In the pedestal's shadow was a large, oval-shaped, rock. What was it doing in the throne room?

Lauryn twitched, a frown on her face as she stared at it. "I think it's the one I sat on when Ever fell on me. It must've come through the portal with me."

"That's unusual." Uncle Guy moved to examine the grayish-white rock. He was the expert on portals. "Nothing that isn't on the person travels through the portal. You were touching Everard so he came with you. But the portal shouldn't transport inanimate items near you."

The rock moved. Jarell jumped back. Trekker III raced over to sniff it.

"There's a crack in it." Uncle Guy looked puzzled.

Everard poked it with his sword. He startled as it wobbled again.

Trekker III barked, moving backward, then circled around it, cautiously, as if it were alive.

Everard glanced from the dog's reaction to the rock. His face lit up. "Lauryn, it's an egg!"

Allyn blinked. Then it hit him.

Lauryn must've figured it out at the same time. "The firebird's egg! I accidentally brought it back with me."

Staring at his sister, then back at the egg, Allyn realized she had won the quest. "A live bird trumps a feather. You win, Laurie."

He would remain only a prince. He caught Giada staring at him. She looked away when he locked gazes.

A knot formed in his chest. He'd have neither a throne nor the girl he loved.

Lauryn's heart gave a jolt. Awe washed over her as she stared, dumbfounded, at the rocking egg.

A firebird's egg!

It meant the culmination of her dreams. All her hard work learning how to be a good ruler. The lessons in geography, history, and etiquette classes. Tediously studying laws. Listening to courtiers and petitioners when she'd rather be ranging outside with her brothers.

She'd earned her place as the next Reina.

At the disappointment on her twin's face, her triumph dampened.

He'd changed in the last month. Become more responsible. Grown up.

She glanced from Allyn to Everard. He wore his stoic face. What did this mean for their future? Everard was a second son of Winterhome's prince. At least no one would expect her to marry Canteor's crown prince, or a ruler's son in Hamleor. That would be one of her siblings' responsibilities.

The big egg started rocking violently. Wobbling wildly now, the crack grew larger. A beak poked through.

Everyone watched in amazement. Trekker III barked crazily until Jarell dragged him away.

Eventually a head followed as the baby bird pushed itself out of the shell. The gray hatchling was the size of a housecat. It chirped as it stumbled around.

Giada, the animal-lover, knelt and spoke soothingly to it.

Father called for the head falconer to be fetched.

The room buzzed with excitement. Everyone spoke at once.

In a little while, the falconer entered. Father gave him an abbreviated version of the bird's appearance. At the falconer's advice, her parents agreed that he'd keep the firebird in the aviary until it was big enough to be released into the mountains, its natural habitat. Valdeor would have its own mythical firebird.

The falconer approached and gently picked up the baby bird with gloved hands.

After the falconer left, Mother commanded their

attention and everyone quieted.

She glanced from one twin to the other, her eyes penetrating. Her gaze landed on the eldest. "Lauryn, you've always expected the crown to pass to you. You worked hard for it. But Allyn seems to satisfy the requirements needed, as well."

Mother focused her gaze on Allyn. "You've had a taste of responsibility, and though you made mistakes, Allyn, you obviously learned from them. I think this means one thing."

Lauryn's stomach flip-flopped in anticipation.

"The crown belongs to both of you. You shall reign together as Rex and Reina, high king and high queen of Valdeor, sharing the burden of ruling."

Lauryn and Allyn's gazes met. A heavy weight lifted from her shoulders as she realized she no longer had to bear the expectations alone. Allyn had always had her back, and that would continue in a different way.

She smiled and he gave her an answering grin.

Lysa threw her arms about Lauryn. Allyria and Allek offered their congratulations.

Jarell put his arms around both of them and squished them. "Nice going. Though you couldn't have done it without my help." He smirked then yelped as they both punched him in the ribs.

Uncle Guy clapped Lauryn on the shoulder before moving away to do the same to Allyn. Aunt Donella gave her a big hug, as did Princess Jiana.

"You'll make a great Reina," Aunt Donella whispered.

"I knew you'd prove yourself worthy." Ever's eyes crinkled as he stepped beside her. "You know you have my support," his voice lowered. "Always and forever." She had a feeling he wanted to say more, but this wasn't the place.

Mother called Jarell forward. He knelt at her feet while she put the medallion around his neck. It glowed with courage, moderation, faith and hope as his prominent virtues. Taking the Crestin sword, she invested him as Duke of Zendira. Her eyes smiled as she announced, "This is your father's ancestral province. Rule it well."

Lauryn considered how if she or her twin had lost, this would have been the reward. But since she and Allyn were equal rulers, it fell to Jarell.

He beamed with pride and importance. "I'll do my best to be a wise leader."

Her parents smiled at Jarell. Everyone congratulated him.

When they quieted, Father coughed, pulling attention to himself. "Let's not forget Prince Everard. In his devotion to the royal family, he was willing to give up his life for my daughter."

All eyes turned on Everard. His cheeks burned crimson.

"What boon will you ask?"

Everard opened his mouth but nothing came out. He quickly glanced at Lauryn, then away.

Lauryn huffed under her breath. She knew what she

wanted him to say. He could be bold against a slew of pirates. Face down a wild boar. Fight twenty men to get to her side. But he was tongue-tied when it came to speaking his feelings.

Happiness slipped through her fingers.

Father grinned. Ever's bashfulness seemed to amuse him. "Then I will offer you a reward. Winterhome has always been a great ally. And you have proved your worth time and time again. Would you like my daughter Lauryn's hand in marriage?"

Adam's apple bobbing, Ever rasped, "Yes, very much, Your Highness. Your Majesty." He sketched a bow towards her parents. "I care deeply for your daughter. I always have." He turned to Lauryn, his hazel eyes crinkling at the corners. "But it took nearly dying for me to know the depth of my heart."

Aunt Donella clapped and winked at Lauryn. Everyone took up clapping as Everard reached out and took Lauryn's hand in his. His grasp was firm. Her pulse zinged.

She felt giddy with emotion. The crown. Her twin ruling beside her. Now, the man of her dreams.

As everyone mingled, discussing events, Everard leaned close and whispered. "I was afraid of change in our relationship. I didn't want to risk something more only to lose your friendship."

"I always had a crush on you," she admitted.

"I guessed that. But I feared you'd grow out of it and regret being emotionally attached to a second son. You were the heir to Valdeor's throne, the crown princess. I didn't want your heart tangled with mine." His voice grew husky. "I thought your mother would insist on an alliance beyond Valdeor's borders."

"I feared that, too." She bit her lip, then gushed, "You're the only one I can be myself with, outside of my family." She blushed, then smiled at him mischievously. "Besides, you can't live without me. Your life would be too boring. I'm not intimidated by your stoic attitude."

"Nor my criticisms, nor my teasing?" He quirked an eyebrow at her.

"Not even your bossiness."

"Nothing, it seems, intimidates you." His eyes twinkled and he squeezed her hand.

19 Birthday Party

The twin's eighteenth birthday finally arrived.

Allyn and Lauryn stood on the steps of the dais in the throne room. They dressed in matching outfits of deep purple. A seven-pointed star embroidered in gold thread adorned their sleeves and hems. A golden sash crossed the chest of his tunic. Lauryn's square-necked dress was cinched with a golden belt. Heavy gold crowns, encrusted with jewels in the seven colors of virtue, weighed on their heads.

They graciously accepted congratulations from the nobles after the hours-long coronation ceremony naming them joint heirs. Nothing like it had happened in Valdeor's recorded history. He bore the title crown prince and his sister was still the crown princess. When Mother passed, he would become Rex and Lauryn would become Reina.

According to Mother, the virtues of their firstborn children would decide which one would succeed them as Valdeor's heir, because they would be of the same rank, no matter birth order. The heartstone medallion would shine brightest for the future ruler, whether boy or girl, Allyn's or

Lauryn's.

Lauryn glowed as she received many congratulations on her engagement.

As they finished greeting the last noble, Allyn and Lauryn sat together on their thrones in the place of honor, at Mother's left. Their siblings were to Father's right.

They looked out over the assembled crowd, now mingling.

Lauryn leaned over so only Allyn could hear, "What's going on between you and Giada? I thought she would be at your side." She glanced over where Everard hovered, near enough to call, but far enough away not to listen in on their conversation. He intercepted her glance, and winked at her.

"I thought so too." Allyn couldn't keep the disappointment from his voice. "I told her I would marry her. I expected her to be overjoyed. I really thought we had a connection, you know? But she ran away crying." Allyn glanced with a heavy heart at the object of their conversation.

Across the room, Giada looked equally sorrowful.

"Ever since that day, I've tried speaking to her, but she's stayed in her suite with her parents. She won't answer my messages, or Prince Gensard didn't pass them along." He sighed. An ache pierced his chest, sharp as a dagger point, as he watched a handsome young man approach Giada and speak to her.

"Did you tell her you love her?"

Allyn startled, looking sheepish. "Well, not in so many

words. She must know how I feel." He spread his hands apart. "I've made it obvious for weeks."

Lauryn rolled her eyes. "She probably thinks you offered for her to save her reputation. You know, out of a sense of duty, because you want to do the right thing, the noble thing." She wagged a finger at him. "Girls need to hear the words."

Allyn frowned.

The young nobleman departed. Giada stood apart with her father.

Allyn stood and squared his shoulders. He walked over and addressed Prince Gensard. "Your Highness, I love your daughter and would like to enter into a marriage alliance with her. She'll have every advantage as a royal consort." He risked a peek at her. "I'll do everything in my power to make her happy."

Giada's eyes had widened when he declared his feelings. Now, she raised her eyes to his, shyly.

He drew his gaze away from her reluctantly, and faced her father. "I know she's only sixteen now. But I'm willing to be betrothed until you think she is old enough to enter the bonds of matrimony."

Giada's face lit up. She turned pleading eyes on her father. Her mother, Princess Jiana, came over. She glanced between their faces, rightly guessing the subject of their conversation. She laid her arm across Giada's shoulders, adding her weight to the side of the youths.

Prince Gensard wavered. He glanced at Mother where she sat on her throne watching the proceedings. As if she knew what transpired, she turned her eyes on them.

Allyn had spoken with his parents on several occasions, explaining his feelings. They no longer had objections, now that Lauryn would reign with him. Samarantha and Winterhome alliances were more important than ones across the sea. Both marriages would strengthen Valdeor internally.

Mother beckoned Allyn, Giada and her parents to approach.

Allyn took the chance to whisper to Giada, as they followed in her parents' wake. "I'm not marrying you just to save your reputation. Surely, you know I've loved you all this time?"

"I wasn't sure." Giada slipped her hand into his. "You were forced to gallantly rescue me, time and again. I've been nothing but a burden."

"Not true. You helped me realize my responsibilities to those I love, as well as my citizens. I couldn't have done it without you." He squeezed her fingers, and her smile lit up her face. He grinned back.

Allyn bowed before his mother. Giada curtsied beside him.

"Samarantha has always been a valuable ally to the throne." Even pale and ill, Mother's eyes were sharp with intelligence. Wrapped in a purple cloak lined in black fur and wearing an elaborate crown upon her chestnut hair, she exuded power. "You wanted our families to merge at one time, Gensard." They shared a glance of unspoken meaning.

The proud prince looked away first. He reached for his wife's hand and entwined their fingers.

Allyn knew Giada's father would capitulate when his gaze rested fondly on his daughter. "Very well. Giada's happiness is paramount to her mother and me. We can discuss terms later."

Giada gave a cry and hugged her father.

She turned toward Allyn shyly. He opened his arms and she snuggled against him. For a moment he enjoyed holding her. Then, becoming aware of their surroundings, he let his hands drop until he snagged the fingers of one of her hands. "You've made me the happiest man alive. I will find ways to show you my love every day of our lives."

Allyn won his love after all.

Lauryn, grinning, joined him, Everard in tow.

Mother announced Allyn's betrothal to those assembled. When the cheering quieted down, she bade everyone to join them in a celebratory feast of the twins' eighteenth birthday and of their succession to the throne. And, now, two engagements.

Father picked Mother up as if she weighed nothing, leading the procession from the throne room.

Prince Gensard gently tugged on his wife's hand, drawing her attention away from Allyn and Giada. His soon-to-be in-laws strolled behind Allyn's parents.

Lauryn followed, hooking her arm around Everard's.

Allyn bowed over Giada's hand. She giggled, nervously. He took her hand and tucked it under the crook of his elbow, leading his beloved forward.

The future spread out rosily before them.

Acknowledgments

I wish to thank my editors: Susan Peek, author of God's Forgotten Friends, who also happens to be my sister; and Margie Cichoke for all their insights. My illustrator: Emily Hickman, who created the beautiful cover and is wonderful to work with. My husband Tom who encourages me to keep writing as long as I have stories to tell. My mother who instilled in me the love of reading. And all my readers who ask when my next book is coming out.

About the Author

Sandra Hanley spent her childhood making up stories and illustrating them. An avid reader, she has devoured about 3000 books in many genres. She taught elementary school for eight years, and middle school for five.

She lives in beautiful Inland Northwest with her husband. Her hobbies are painting, crocheting, reading, writing and dreaming up imaginary worlds.

Be sure to sign up for her newsletter at www.sandralena-hanley.com for upcoming stories in the Royal Rescue series, as well as the Valdeor Chronicles for tweens and teens.

If you enjoyed this story, please consider helping the author by rating it on Amazon and Goodreads.

BOOK 4 OF THE VALDEOR CHRONICLES

Princess Lauryn always expected to be the heir to Valdeor's throne. Now she finds herself in a race against her twin brother Allyn to discover the whereabouts of the legendary firebird. Showing virtues on the quest will win her place as the next Reina.

Prince Allyn has never coveted the crown nor the responsibilities that go with it. But he must become a leader when he finds himself in dangerous territory with his younger brother and the pretty princess of Samarantha under his care.

Apart, the twins face foes on faraway shores, heartbreak, and betrayal. Can they reunite, tackle the firebird, and save Valdeor from the machinations of a foreign prince?

Also available from this author
· Champions of Valdeor
· Waykeepers of Valdeor
· Pilgrims of Valdeor

ISBN 9781737739845

90000

9 781737 739845